Llewelyn, David

SF
DOCTOR
34   Doctor Who
        Che...   P9-DGJ-590
        Doctor Who: New Series
        Adventures ; 34

DISCARDED
on public Library

HURON PUBLIC LIBRARY
521 DAKOTA AVE S
HURON, SD 57350

DOCTOR·WHO

The Taking of Chelsea 426

Fic
Dr. Who
Taking

DOCTOR·WHO

The Taking
of
Chelsea 426

DAVID LLEWELLYN

B·**B**·**C**
BOOKS

HURON PUBLIC LIBRARY
521 DAKOTA AVE S
HURON, SD 57350

2 4 6 8 10 9 7 5 3 1

Published in 2009 by BBC Books, an imprint of Ebury Publishing
A Random House Group Company

© David Llewellyn, 2009

David Llewellyn has asserted his right to be identified as the author of this
Work in accordance with the Copyright, Design and Patents Act 1988.

Doctor Who is a BBC Wales production for BBC One
Executive Producers: Russell T Davies and Julie Gardner

Original series broadcast on BBC Television. Format © BBC 1963.
'Doctor Who', 'TARDIS' and the Doctor Who logo are trademarks of the
British Broadcasting Corporation and are used under licence.
Sontarans created by Robert Holmes. Rutans created by Terrance Dicks.

All rights reserved. No part of this publication may be reproduced,
stored in a retrieval system, or transmitted in any form or by any means,
electronic, mechanical, photocopying, recording or otherwise, without
the prior permission of the copyright owner.

The Random House Group Ltd Reg. No. 954009.
Addresses for companies within the Random House Group can be found
at www.randomhouse.co.uk.

A CIP catalogue record for this book is available from the British
Library.

ISBN 978 1 846 07758 6

The Random House Group Limited supports the Forest Stewardship
Council (FSC), the leading international forest certification organisation.
All our titles that are printed on Greenpeace approved FSC certified
paper carry the FSC logo. Our paper procurement policy can be found
at www.rbooks.co.uk/environment

Series Consultant: Justin Richards
Project Editor: Steve Tribe
Cover design by Lee Binding © BBC 2009

Typeset in Albertina and Deviant Strain
Printed and bound in Germany by GGP Media GmbH

For Jake Bennett, Ella Moggridge, and Jacob Llewellyn –
saviours of the universe

Alice Wendell stepped out beneath the great glass dome of the Oxygen Gardens and gazed up to see the glittering, icy moon of Tethys passing overhead.

She had lived on Chelsea 426 for almost six months, practically since her graduation, but still the other residents – and even her colleagues – looked at her and spoke to her as if she were a complete stranger. She was sure they meant nothing by it, of course; it was just their way.

Even her boss, Professor Wilberforce, addressed her in such a clipped and formal manner you might think they had only just met, and not that they had worked together almost every day since her arrival.

But then, the Professor had lived on the colony longer than anyone else. He had arrived when it first opened as a part of the Interplanetary Mining Corporation's first hydrogen mine on Saturn. Back then his role had been to maintain the Oxygen Gardens, a job he still carried out, though the mine had long since closed and the colony had become the property of Powe-Luna Developments.

It was they who had changed the name of the colony from Unit 426 to Chelsea 426, and they who had refurbished it completely, transforming it from a utilitarian domicile into a close approximation of a twentieth-century English market town.

Within the airtight confines of the colony there were gardens and tree-lined streets filled with shops, offices, schools and the occasional church. Outside, the colony resembled a raft cobbled together from barrels, though in the case of Chelsea 426 each 'barrel' was roughly the same size as a tower block. Flanking the raft of units that made up the colony were colossal, semi-translucent discs, each more than a mile in diameter, which reminded Alice of water lily pads. It was these discs, as well as the colony's fusion candle, that kept it floating on the surface of Saturn's gas clouds.

On the morning of 20 August, the gardens were a hive of activity, with botanists dashing this way and that, making all the last-minute preparations and adjustments before the grand opening of the Flower Show. With every passing day, more and more guests were arriving, and anticipation for the unveiling of the plants had reached feverish levels.

After a moment's pause, and a deep breath, Alice walked across the gardens to where Professor Wilberforce was standing at the foot of the largest specimen, a creation he had named *Caeruliflora Saturnalis*, the 'Blue Flower of Saturn'.

It was a giant of a plant, nearly four metres in height, its thick trunk rising high above a cluster of palmate leaves before erupting into one colossal blue blossom. Scattered in the flowerbeds around its base were numerous other shrubs and bushes, none of them recognisable as any earthly plant.

Alice had seen and studied extraterrestrial flora before at university, but this was the first time that any such plant life had been discovered within the boundaries of the solar system. Though the promise of a flower show might not have seemed an exciting invitation, the promise of *alien* plants was. Thousands were expected to pass through the doors of the Oxygen Gardens in the coming week, and thousands had, indeed, already arrived, making the journey to Saturn from all across the solar system.

As Alice crossed the gardens towards the Professor, she was carelessly knocked sideways by a colleague who was too focused on scribbling into a notebook to see where he was going.

'Scuse me!' said the botanist, seconds after he had passed her.

Alice straightened her lab coat and her glasses, took a deep breath, and carried on until she reached the Professor.

'Er, Professor Wilberforce,' she said, sheepishly. 'I… I was wondering if I could have a word?'

Professor Wilberforce turned to her and for a moment said nothing, simply staring at her with no trace of emotion.

'That would be agreeable,' he said, eventually. 'You seem somewhat perturbed. Is something the matter?'

Alice nodded, nervously straightening her glasses once more.

'Um, yes,' she said awkwardly. 'I've been monitoring the atmospheric readings and I've noticed that, er, the, er…'

'Spit it out, girl,' snapped Wilberforce. 'I haven't got all day.'

'Well, I'm getting a high reading of ammonia.'

Wilberforce nodded thoughtfully, tapping the end of his pen against his teeth.

'Ammonia, you say?'

Alice nodded, her chin in her chest.

'Well that's interesting,' the Professor continued. 'Very interesting indeed. Follow me to my office. I'm sure there's a perfectly rational explanation for all this.'

'Of course,' said Alice, following the Professor as he left the main chamber of the gardens and walked down the narrow corridor toward his office.

Entering the Professor's office was like stepping into another era. The walls were decorated with wooden panels on which the Professor's many certificates and qualifications hung in frames. One wall of the room was occupied exclusively with bookshelves crammed from end to end with leather-bound volumes. His mahogany desk was huge and furnished with a large antique globe and a Tiffany dragonfly lamp.

In one dimly lit corner of the office, under a glass dome, he kept a smaller specimen of *Caeruliflora Saturnalis*, an almost bonsai-scaled replica of the giant in the main chamber.

As Alice neared the centre of the room, Professor Wilberforce closed the door behind her.

'Now, Alice,' he said, his tone suddenly warmer, more genial. 'Why do you think there might be a noticeable trace of ammonia in the main chamber?'

'W-w-well,' she stuttered. 'I don't… I don't know. The environment here is controlled one hundred per cent. There shouldn't be *any* traces of ammonia in there. Unless… unless the plants are producing it, but we've—'

'Already tested for that?'

'Well yes. So the only thing I can… um… think is that—'

'Somebody is leaking ammonia into the chamber?'

'Er… yes.'

Professor Wilberforce clapped his hands together just

once, beaming at Alice as if she were suddenly his star pupil. She had never seen him behave this way before. It left her feeling strangely uncomfortable.

'Quite right,' said Wilberforce. 'Quite right. A trace of ammonia *is* being fed into the chamber. Fed, Alice. Not leaked.' He walked across the office to the glass dome containing the smaller plant. 'They really are a miracle, aren't they?'

Alice nodded with what she hoped looked like enthusiasm, though she still felt uneasy.

'All this,' said the Professor. 'This sudden fruition, this glorious outburst of life, and all from the tiniest of spores.'

'Y-yes,' said Alice.

'How many years must the spores have been waiting there, Alice, do you think? Centuries? Millennia, perhaps? Who can say? All those years, those tiny, almost microscopic spores floated in the turbulence of the planet's atmosphere, still alive but without the right environment to thrive. How do you think they survived, Alice?'

Alice looked from Professor Wilberforce to the plant and back again, shrugging.

'They were alive the whole time,' said Wilberforce. 'Living breathing organisms, floating in clouds of hydrogen, helium… and ammonia.'

Alice looked up, her eyes growing wide behind the lenses of her glasses.

'They breathe ammonia?'

Professor Wilberforce beamed once more.

'My dear girl,' he said, 'you clever thing. They *breathe* ammonia. But only the spores. For the plants to truly thrive they need so many other elements. Ultraviolet light, carbon dioxide… All the things that earthly plants require.'

Now Alice frowned.

'But that doesn't make sense. Why would a plant develop on Saturn that could only survive in its spore form?'

Professor Wilberforce smiled and nodded without answering her question. He lifted the glass dome away from the plant.

At once Alice could smell it: the same faint unpleasant whiff of ammonia that had first led her to check the readings from the chamber.

'But,' said Professor Wilberforce, 'what if the plant did not develop on Saturn? What if it was developed elsewhere?'

Alice nodded thoughtfully, trying hard not to wince at the unpleasant smell.

'Well we have discussed exogenesis,' she said, placing the back of her hand over her nose. 'They may have arrived here on a comet, or a meteorite. They could have come from another planet.'

'Well done,' said Professor Wilberforce, still grinning from ear to ear.

'But you said *developed*,' said Alice. 'What do you mean?'

Professor Wilberforce gestured toward her with one hand, beckoning her closer to the plant.

'Come here,' he said, still smiling warmly. 'A little closer, if you will. That's it. Lean closer. What if the plant were developed elsewhere, and designed to fulfil a purpose?'

Alice leaned close to the plant, studying its azure petals and its snaking, almost reptilian stem.

'What if,' the Professor continued, 'its restive state would only require it to breathe ammonia, waiting very patiently for the day when others might discover it?'

'Others?' asked Alice, turning to the Professor. 'You mean us?'

Wilberforce nodded.

'Yes,' he said, still smiling. 'You.'

'I'm sorry, but I don't know what you m—'

Before she could finish her sentence the blue flower spat out a small but dense cloud of heavily perfumed green dust, the particles so fine it looked almost like smoke.

Alice breathed in sharply, coughing and spluttering and clutching at her throat. She tried to speak but couldn't; her throat felt as if it were getting narrower and narrower. Coloured lights danced before her eyes and the room began to spin.

Professor Wilberforce hooked his arm around her

and carried her to a chair, placing her down gently. Everything around her was beginning to lose focus; the office, the desk, the Professor. The room was getting darker and the Professor's voice echoed as if he were very far away.

'There there,' she heard him say as she was swallowed by the darkness. 'It will all be over in a moment.'

Minutes later, Alice Wendell and Professor Wilberforce were standing in the main chamber of the gardens, at the foot of the *Caeruliflora Saturnalis*.

'We weren't expecting *humans*,' she said, with disdain.

'No,' said Professor Wilberforce with a sigh. 'We weren't. It would appear our enemies are not the only ones mining hydrogen in this sector.'

'How many of us are there now?' Alice asked.

'A few,' replied the Professor. 'Not many, but soon there will be visitors. Thousands of visitors.'

'Thousands?' said Alice, turning to Wilberforce and grinning malevolently.

'Oh yes,' he told her, returning the smile. 'Thousands.'

ONE

Jake Carstairs looked out at the ink-black canvas of space and waited. He pressed his nose against the cold glass, his every breath fogging up the window a little more than the last, and he waited.

Eventually it came into view, the colossal cylindrical hulk of the hotel pod, its retro rockets firing out streams of gas. There were people in the windows, little more than silhouettes against the interior lights of the hotel; guests and hotel staff, he imagined. He wondered whether any of them were looking down at his parents' guest house just as he was looking up at them.

Slowly, and with surprising grace for an object nearly a hundred metres in length, the hotel pod turned and aligned itself with the westernmost wing of the colony.

HURON PUBLIC LIBRARY
521 DAKOTA AVE S
HURON, SD 57350

Beyond the western wing and the hotel pod, the surface of the planet stretched out like a vast and seemingly infinite desert, neatly cut in two, to the south, by the shadow of the rings.

The hotel pod was now surrounded by tug craft, pulling it in closer to the docking platforms. Hydraulic arms reached out and fastened themselves to the hull of the pod until it finally came to rest.

'Another one?'

It was the voice of Jake's sister, Vienna. More than just his sister, Vienna was his twin, born less than twenty minutes before him nearly fourteen years ago. He didn't turn to see her expression, but from her tone he could sense what sounded like disappointment.

'Yeah,' he said. 'Another one.'

'How many more do you think there'll be?' asked Vienna.

Jake turned and shrugged.

'I dunno,' he said. 'Depends how many people are coming, doesn't it?'

Vienna nodded.

They were standing in room 237 of their parents' guest house, the Grand Hotel, the only permanent hotel on the colony. Strictly speaking, neither of them should have been there, their parents forever fearful they might break something or disrupt the orderly tidiness.

Jake only ever came to the upper-level rooms when there were ships arriving, like the hotel pods. He'd liked watching them dock ever since the family had first arrived on Chelsea 426, almost two years ago. It was one of the few things about the colony that he *did* like.

'Dad won't be happy,' said Vienna.

'No,' said Jake. 'Mum neither.'

'We'd better go back downstairs before they realise we're up here, or we'll be in serious trouble.'

Jake nodded dolefully and followed his sister out of the room.

Away from the viewing windows of the guest rooms, the Grand Hotel could easily have been anywhere in the galaxy. It could even have been back on Earth. There was something very old fashioned about the corridors, the doors, even the carpets that would have seemed quite out of place on a floating colony, were it not for the fact that virtually all of Chelsea 426 was decorated that way. Even the emergency escape hatches, enormous circular doors that opened out directly into the black void of space, were hidden behind plush velvet curtains. The paintings on the walls depicted scenes from a half-forgotten world of rolling fields, fox hunts, and rural hamlets.

Jake often wondered whether the world, or at least the world back home, had ever looked like the one depicted in the paintings. He doubted it, somehow.

With fixed concentration, Mr Carstairs cleaned the faint oily thumbprint from his spectacles and held them up to the light. Blown up larger than life and distorted by the curvature of the lenses, the hull of the hotel pod made its way silently and gracefully across the upper windows of the lobby and towards the Western Docks of Chelsea 426. Mr Carstairs sighed and put his glasses back on.

'All right, dear?' asked his wife, Mrs Carstairs, as she stepped out of their office and into the lobby.

'Yes, dear,' said Mr Carstairs. 'Mustn't grumble.'

Mustn't grumble. That was what he said almost every time anyone asked him how he was these days. Mustn't grumble. He'd usually say it with a cheery smile or a noncommittal shrug, as if it were just another throwaway saying, but he knew deep down that 'mustn't grumble' was his way of saying he hadn't had a decent night's sleep in weeks.

Mustn't grumble.

So-so.

Not too bad.

Standing at his side, Mrs Carstairs followed her husband's gaze up to the lobby windows and saw the hotel pod in the few brief seconds before it disappeared from view.

'Another one?' she asked.

Her husband nodded.

'With guests already on board, I imagine,' she continued, sighing softly.

'Most likely,' said Mr Carstairs.

'Lots of *Newcomers*.'

'Undoubtedly.'

The Grand Hotel had a hundred and fifty guest rooms, and only one of them was occupied. When the Mayor and Professor Wilberforce at the Oxygen Gardens had first announced the Flower Show, the Carstairs had celebrated. Finally, they had thought, an opportunity to make a decent living here on Chelsea 426. The Flower Show would bring guests, and the guests would bring money.

They hadn't counted on the Newcomers and the hotel pods. Why should the glitterati of the solar system spend their time at the colony in an old-fashioned and slightly threadbare hotel when they could be transported there in six- and seven-star luxury? Wherever the money from the Flower Show was going, it certainly hadn't ended up in the pockets of Mr and Mrs Carstairs.

'I suppose we'd better get started on the dining room,' said Mrs Carstairs with another sigh.

'I thought I'd ask the children,' said Mr Carstairs. 'Keep them busy and out of trouble.'

'Good idea,' said Mrs Carstairs, smiling weakly. 'Talking of which, where are they?'

As if to answer her question, the elevator doors opened, and Jake and Vienna stepped out.

'And what were you two doing upstairs?' asked Mr Carstairs, his eyebrows bunched together, giving him the appearance of an aggravated owl.

'Nothing,' said Jake. 'Just… Nothing.'

'I *do* hope you weren't in any of the rooms,' said his mother. 'I only finished cleaning the windows yesterday. If I find any of your grubby little fingerprints…'

'Quite,' said Mr Carstairs, tutting and shaking his head. 'What were you doing, son? Looking at all the spaceships again, were you? There's no good ever came from daydreaming about spaceships. And what about you?' He turned to Vienna.

'Nothing,' she replied. 'I was just looking for Jake.'

'Right,' said Mr Carstairs. 'I see. Well why don't the two of you pop down to Mr Pemberton's and buy me a few tins of furniture polish? We've still got the dining room to do and we've run out.'

'OK, Dad,' said Jake.

Mr Carstairs took out his wallet and was thumbing out banknotes when the sliding doors of the hotel's entrance hissed open, and a stranger walked in.

He was a tall man in a blue suit, shirt and tie, but on his feet he wore a pair of very old-fashioned, burgundy-coloured shoes. The kind people used to call 'trainers'.

'Oh, hello!' the man said, beaming at the four of them. 'Is this a hotel, then?'

Mr and Mrs Carstairs looked from the stranger to the large sign behind the reception desk that read *The Grand Hotel*, and then back to the stranger.

'Yes,' said Mr Carstairs, somewhat sardonically. 'It is.'

'*Molto bene!*' said the stranger. 'Just the ticket. Got any rooms?'

Jake and Vienna looked at one another and then to their father. His expression had faded from one of haughty derision to tired resignation.

'Yes,' said Mr Carstairs with a sigh. 'We have plenty of rooms.'

He walked round to the other side of the reception desk and opened the leather-bound guest book, producing a fountain pen from his pocket.

'Just the single room?' he asked, peering up at the stranger over his half-moon glasses.

'Yes, just the one,' said the stranger, looking around at the hotel lobby. 'Just little old me, myself and I. All by my lonesome. Nobody here but us chickens, et cetera.'

Jake smiled and briefly caught the stranger's gaze. The stranger winked at him and then returned his attention to Mr Carstairs, who seemed far from amused by the stranger's behaviour.

'Could I take your name?' he asked impatiently.

'Yes. The Doctor.'

There was a long silence. Mr Carstairs held the pen's nib an inch above the paper but wrote nothing.

'The Doctor?' he asked eventually.

'That's right,' said the stranger, still beaming.

'I'll need your full name,' said Mr Carstairs. 'Unless your first name is "the"…?'

'Oh, right. Yes. Course. Smith.'

'Smith?'

'Yup.'

'First name?'

'John.'

'John… Smith?'

'Yup.'

Mr Carstairs audibly huffed through his nose, but still didn't write anything in the book.

'I don't suppose there will be a *Mrs* Smith turning up at any point, unannounced, now will there?' said Mrs Carstairs, leaning into the stranger's field of view.

'Oh no,' said the stranger, his smile breaking just a little. 'No. Like I said, it's just me.'

'Doctor… John… Smith…' said Mr Carstairs, finally writing it down. 'Do you have any luggage, Doctor Smith?'

'Oh no,' said the Doctor still looking everywhere except at Mr Carstairs. 'No… Travel light. That's my motto. Well… One of my mottos. One of several, actually. Can you have *several* mottos?'

There was a brief pause, as if Mr Carstairs were waiting to make sure the Doctor had finished speaking.

'And do you have any specific dietary requirements?' he asked, eventually.

'Oh no,' said the Doctor. 'Except pears. Can't stand pears.'

'No… pears…' said Mr Carstairs, jotting down one last note in the book.

Once he had logged their new guest's details and taken payment for the room, Mr Carstairs handed over a key card, and wished the Doctor good day.

As the Doctor made his way toward the elevators, Mr Carstairs handed Jake a single banknote.

'There's ten there. Get me four tins of polish, and don't go dawdling. You'll need to get to work on those tables by five o'clock. The pair of you.'

Jake and Vienna nodded dolefully and were on their way out through the sliding doors when the Doctor about-turned and caught up with them.

'Are these your kids?' he asked Mr Carstairs.

'Yes…' replied Mr Carstairs, somewhat hesitantly.

'Right, only I'm not from round these parts and was looking for a tour guide. Mind if I tag along with them? See the sights?'

Mr Carstairs turned to his wife and shrugged.

'I don't see why not,' said Mrs Carstairs, casting a vaguely suspicious eye over the stranger. 'As long as they are back by five. They have chores.'

'They will be,' said the stranger. 'Wouldn't want to keep two children from their chores, now, would I?'

Jake and Vienna looked at one another and shrugged in unison before stepping out onto the long, metal walkway of Tunbridge Street, accompanied by their new guest.

Once the doors had closed behind them, Jake turned and looked up at the stranger.

'Your name's not really John Smith, is it?' he asked.

'Nope,' said the stranger with a smile.

'So what *is* your name?' asked Vienna.

'The Doctor,' replied the stranger.

'Yeah, but Doctor what?'

'Oh, just the Doctor. What's your name?'

'I'm Jake,' answered Jake.

'And I'm Vienna.'

'Ooh,' said the Doctor. 'After the city or the song?'

Vienna frowned.

'Never mind,' the Doctor continued. 'Nice to meet you, Jake and Vienna. I'm the Doctor. Oh… Already done that bit. Right… Which way are we going?'

Shaking their heads and rolling their eyes, Jake and Vienna led the Doctor down Tunbridge Street. Though it was called a 'street', it was little more than a corridor, and a very crowded one at that. People were shuffling in both directions, dragging suitcases and barking orders at their families to 'keep up'.

'Lots of visitors, then?' said the Doctor. 'Must be busy at the hotel.'

'Not really,' Jake told him. 'They've got these hotel pods. Brand new ones. Newer than our hotel.'

'Shh, Jake,' said Vienna. 'You know Dad doesn't like it if we talk like that.'

Eventually they came to Miramont Gardens, a wide square lined with silver birches and flanked on each side by rows of shops. In the centre of the square were rows of brightly coloured flowerbeds arranged around a small fountain.

Like Tunbridge Street, Miramont Gardens was bustling with people. Some were recognisable as residents of the colony, the children dressed in short trousers, dresses and polished shoes, the adults in sensible tweeds, but most of the people there looked like tourists, many of them snapping away with their cameras and pointing at the residents as if they were animals in a zoo.

'Look at them!' said a large woman in a big pink hat, as she bustled past with her equally large family in tow. 'They're all so cute!'

Jake and Vienna were the only residents who weren't dressed as if they had come from the 1900s.

'So,' said the Doctor, craning back his head and looking up at the high curved ceiling of the pod, barely visible beyond the glare of a hundred artificial suns. 'This is Chelsea 426, then?'

'Yes,' said Jake.

'Hmm,' the Doctor continued. 'Very post-modern.'

He looked to the children for approval but met only blank faces.

'So how long is it since you were last on Earth?' he asked.

'Two years,' said Jake and Vienna, in unison.

'Ooh, make a wish,' said the Doctor.

Again, the twins frowned.

'It's a saying. When you say something at the same time as somebody… Oh, never mind. So *two years*, eh? Two years all the way out here on Saturn?'

Vienna nodded, rolling her eyes.

'Someone's not impressed!' said the Doctor, grinning. 'And how about you, Jake? How are you enjoying life here in Boring-Upon-Twee?'

Both children laughed, quickly covering their mouths with their hands as if afraid somebody might hear.

'Well, I can see why,' said the Doctor. 'I mean, it's very *nice* and everything, but… I don't know… It's all a bit samey, isn't it? Like one great big… *jamboree* of samey-ness. Two teenagers, out here, in Quaintsville? What do you lot do for a laugh?'

Their smiles fading, Jake and Vienna looked at one another and then back at the Doctor, both frowning.

'You know,' said the Doctor. 'What kind of mischief do you get up to? I mean, there must be somewhere you all hang out? Playing your music and scaring the oldies, or whatever it is kids do these days…'

Jake shook his head. 'Not really,' he said. 'We just help out at the hotel. And we go to school.'

'What?' said the Doctor, and then more insistently. '*What?* But that's *ridiculous.* You mean to say there's nowhere on Chelsea 426 for kids to just muck about and make little nuisances of themselves?'

Vienna laughed, shaking her head.

'No,' she said. 'That's strictly against the rules.'

'Oh,' said the Doctor, his tone sarcastically sincere. 'And what rules would *they* be?'

'The Colony Code,' said Jake.

'What's that when it's at home?' asked the Doctor. 'Is it anything like the Highway Code? The *bar*code? The Da Vinci Code?'

'The *Colony* Code,' repeated Vienna. 'The rules for living on the colony.'

'Number one,' said Jake. 'No loud music utilising repetitive beats or lyrics of a lewd or lascivious nature.'

'Number two,' said his sister. 'No clothing of an unnecessarily ostentatious or revealing manner to be worn at any time.'

'Number three. No public drunkenness.'

'Number four. No public displays of excessive affection, e.g. open-mouthed kissing…'

Jake giggled.

'… Or fondling of any kind.'

'Number five,' said Jake. 'No bawdy humour or foul language.'

'And number six,' concluded Vienna. 'No gatherings of children between the hours of 4 p.m. and 8 a.m.'

The Doctor nodded sagely.

'Is that all?' he asked. 'So, basically, in a nutshell, if you had to summarise the Colony Code, it's "Thou shalt not have fun"?'

'Yeah,' said Vienna, laughing. 'More or less.'

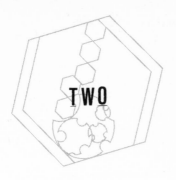

TWO

'**H**ello!' squawked the mynah bird, landing on its swing. 'Hello!'

'Hello yourself,' grumbled Mr Pemberton as he carried four tins of paint from the stockroom to the shop floor. He handed them to Wallace Fitch, his 15-year-old assistant, whose skinny frame sagged from the sudden weight. 'There you go. Top shelf, next to the varnish. And then I want you to empty the mousetraps in the scullery. Honestly… Mice… They'll get anywhere. Here we are a billion miles from Earth and we still get blimmin' mice.'

Wallace nodded obediently as he climbed the stepladder, his paint-tin-laden arms shaking at his sides.

'And don't drop 'em,' said Mr Pemberton, chuckling softly to himself.

Once Wallace had placed each tin of paint on the shelf, the ladder wobbling and rattling beneath him, he stepped down and scurried back into the stockroom, his head bowed, leaving his boss alone on the shop floor.

Mr Pemberton was a tall, portly man, his thinning hair pomaded over the dome of his bald head. He was only very rarely out of his shirt, tie and white apron, and in the pocket of his apron there were always three pens: one black, one blue, one red.

His was the oldest hardware shop on Chelsea 426. He and Mrs Pemberton had emigrated only a few months after the colony had first opened to the public.

Truth be told, they'd had enough of Earth. Not long before their departure, Mrs Pemberton had had what they'd called 'a spot of bother' with a gang of teenagers, and her purse had been stolen. Shortly after that, their shop had been vandalised and its windows broken. The town in which they lived had seemed so much noisier and more aggressive than it had been when, as newlyweds, they'd first moved there.

The world had changed without anyone asking them if they wanted it to.

Life on Chelsea 426 could hardly have been more different. People greeted one another in the street; everyone left their doors unlocked; and the children knew to speak only when spoken to. It was a simple way of life compared to the hustle and the bustle of Earth, but they liked it that way.

Mr Pemberton was back in the stockroom stacking boxes of nails when he heard the bell above the door jangle and the mynah bird flapping its wings. He walked back out into the shop to see the Carstairs children from the Grand Hotel and a tall, thin stranger in a dark blue suit. He greeted Jake and Vienna with a cheery 'good morning', but his expression soured as his eyes met the stranger's.

'Good morning,' he said, phrasing it almost as a question.

'Morning!' said the stranger with a cheerful smile.

'Can I help you?'

'Oh no,' said the stranger, approaching the counter and holding out his hand. 'I'm the Doctor. I'm just tagging along for the ride.'

With a stern nod, Mr Pemberton shook the Doctor's hand, and then turned to Jake and Vienna.

'We need some furniture polish,' said Jake.

Mr Pemberton nodded but didn't take his eyes off this stranger who called himself the Doctor, even as he crossed the shop floor to the shelves of polish.

The Doctor, meanwhile, walked over to the mynah bird's cage and peered in through the bars.

'Hello, there!' he said.

'Hello, there!' said the mynah bird.

'How many was it you needed?' asked Mr Pemberton,

climbing the small stepladder until he was level with the tins of polish.

'Four,' replied Jake.

Mr Pemberton took down four tins and carried them back to the counter.

'That'll be twelve credits,' he said. 'Prices have gone up, sorry.'

'But we've only got a tenner,' said Jake, 'and Dad said we had to get four tins. Can we pay you the other two credits tomorrow?'

Mr Pemberton smiled.

'That would be agreeable,' he said.

'That would be agreeable!' squawked the mynah bird.

The Doctor frowned at the bird and then looked at Mr Pemberton.

'Oh, don't mind him,' said Mr Pemberton. 'He never shuts up.'

'I can imagine,' said the Doctor. 'Not much fun, being stuck in a little cage.'

'Well I've not heard any complaints,' said Mr Pemberton. 'I'm sorry… I didn't properly catch your name. Doctor…?'

'Oh, just the Doctor,' said the Doctor, smiling disarmingly. 'I'm here for the Flower Show. Looking forward to it, in fact. Can't wait.'

Mr Pemberton nodded, still eyeing the Doctor with caution. As he handed Jake the tins in a brown paper bag, Wallace came out from the stockroom and froze in his tracks.

'Oh… er… hello, Vienna,' he said, his voice changing pitch mid-word and his cheeks turning a brighter pink.

'Er… hi, Wallace,' said Vienna, staring at her shoes.

'Oh, hello Vienna,' said Jake in a mocking, squeaky voice, giggling.

Mr Pemberton turned to Wallace with an admonishing glare.

'I hope you've cleaned out them mousetraps!' he barked, and Wallace nodded sheepishly, running back into the stockroom. Mr Pemberton folded the top of the paper bag before handing it to Jake, and in return Jake gave him the money.

The children cheerfully waved goodbye to Mr Pemberton as they walked out of the shop, but the Doctor paused in the open doorway and looked from Mr Pemberton to the mynah bird and back again. He nodded thoughtfully without saying another word, turned and closed the door. With the bell above the doorframe still jangling, the mynah bird squawked, 'Goodbye!'

Mr Pemberton waited a moment before stepping out from behind the counter and walking up to the window. He followed the three of them with a steely glare, and hissed, in a voice barely louder than a whisper, 'The Doctor…'

***

They were halfway across Miramont Gardens when Jake began to sing:

'*Wallace and Vienna in a tree, K.I.S.S.I.N.G…*'

'Shut up!' said Vienna.

The Doctor laughed and then shot Jake a stern look, which the young boy took as a signal to stop singing.

They were on the other side of the Miramont Gardens, near the entrance to Tunbridge Street, when one of the large television screens suspended above the square flashed into life with a fanfare, and the words 'THE SMALLS AGENDA' appeared in big bold letters. The Doctor and the children stopped walking and looked up at the screen, where the letters now faded to reveal a thickset man with a short neck and the gruff expression of a bulldog.

'Hang on a minute,' said the Doctor, squinting up at the screen. 'I've seen him somewhere before…'

'Newcomers,' said the man on the screen with evident distaste. 'Everywhere you look there are Newcomers. You know what I say? They're welcome to visit, but we don't want them to stay, and yet more and more we're hearing about visitors applying for permits to stay here, on Chelsea 426, *after* the Flower Show. Is that what we *really* want?'

'It's Riley Smalls,' said Jake. 'He's on TV all the time.'

'Of course it isn't!' continued Smalls, leaning a little closer to the camera, his face now bunched up in a scowl. 'But what say do we have in the matter? That's right… None whatsoever! Our Mayor is far too busy showing off in front of all our guests to care about what the ordinary man in the street thinks, isn't he? Well I say enough is enough. Do we really want our way of life changed beyond all recognition?'

'But that's impossible,' said the Doctor. 'He was on TV years ago. And I mean *years* ago…'

It was true. On the very few occasions when the Doctor had watched twenty-first-century television he'd encountered that same man, with the same scowl, and the same disgruntled tone of voice. He had been a journalist, in the loosest sense of the word, and the host of his own show, even then.

'Yeah,' said Vienna. 'He's a Cryogen, isn't he?'

The Doctor turned to Vienna, frowning.

'A Cryogen?'

'Don't you know anything? He had something wrong with him, like, five hundred years ago, a tumour or something, so they froze him. They unfroze him about ten years ago, and he came here not long after that.'

The Doctor turned back to the screen and winced.

'Oh, that's not good,' he said.

'Why's that?' asked Jake.

'Long story,' said the Doctor. 'And a bit icky for the under-15s. Maybe some other time. Right now we've got to get you two back in time for your chores.'

The children groaned, and the Doctor ushered them back on to Tunbridge Street.

'So,' he said, as they walked down the covered street, past old women walking their dogs and obedient children following their smartly dressed parents like rows of ducklings, 'Tell me about this Flower Show, then.'

'What's to tell?' asked Jake.

'Well,' said the Doctor. 'Where are the flowers from?'

'You don't know?' said Vienna. 'Have you been living on Pluto for the last year or something?'

'They were in the clouds,' Jake cut in, embarrassed by his sister's sarcasm. 'Just floating around. Professor Wilberforce found them when he was taking samples. He planted them, and they grew into these amazing great big flowers. Only nobody's seen them yet. They won't see them until tomorrow.'

'Right…' said the Doctor. 'And where can I find this Professor Wilberforce?'

THREE

'That's it… If you could just lift your chin a little…
Just like that… Yeah… And hold it… Now try not
to blink… And… Yes.'

Mr Sedgefield, Mayor of Chelsea 426, glanced
sideways at the holographer and huffed loudly through
his nose, rolling his eyes only when the Newcomer
wasn't looking at him.

'Is this going to take much longer?' he asked,
petulantly.

'Oh no,' said the holographer, a scruffily dressed
young man who called himself Zeek. 'Just a few more
shots and we'll be finished.'

If his dress sense alone – torn carellium-weave
trousers and a shimmering neon T-shirt – wasn't enough

to offend, Zeek was also chewing gum. Mr Sedgefield couldn't help but wonder why he hadn't added the chewing of gum to the Colony Code's list of forbidden activities. It certainly wasn't on sale anywhere in Chelsea 426, so the slovenly little tyke must have brought it with him. It would take only a few of the colony's teenagers to see a Newcomer idly chewing gum and soon enough they'd all be doing it.

They were in the Mayoral office, a glass dome at the top of a narrow tower in the heart of the colony. They had been there for some time, with Mr Sedgefield posing in a large wooden chair, an oversized, leather-bound copy of Mark Anthony's *Meditations* open in his lap and tilted at such an angle that the title, embossed on the spine in gold leaf, was visible to Zeek's laser camera. Though the limits of his patience were being tested, the portrait had been Mr Sedgefield's idea in the first place.

It would eventually be shown at an exhibition in the Ubergallery, an enormous man-made island in the North Sea. There the image of Mayor Sedgefield would find itself amongst portraits of the galaxy's 'most influential persons'. On first hearing about the exhibition, Mr Sedgefield had used his contacts back home to ensure he had a place amongst the politicians, entrepreneurs and celebrities.

As Zeek set up the laser camera in another corner of the room, Mr Sedgefield asked, 'Tell me, who will I be next to in the exhibition?'

'I'm sorry?' said Zeek, frowning up at him and still chewing his gum.

'In the exhibition… Whose hologram will be next to mine?'

Zeek shrugged, adjusting the camera and tilting it so that the lens now faced the Mayor directly.

'Dunno,' he said. 'I just take the pictures, innit?'

Mr Sedgefield shook his head in scorn and once more assumed his regal pose, the book open in his lap, but his gaze fixed firmly on the black canopy of space above the dome.

As the camera emitted sudden flashes of green and then red light, there was a knock at the door.

'Come in,' said the Mayor, through gritted teeth, barely opening his mouth, as if he were trying to throw his voice like a ventriloquist.

The door opened very slightly and one of his assistants leaned into the room.

'Mr Mayor,' she said. 'Mr Smalls is here to see you.'

Sedgefield groaned as if he were in some pain, his whole body seeming to deflate. He slammed the weighty, leather-bound volume shut with a loud bang and placed it on his desk. 'Well,' he sighed, 'I suppose you'd better show him in.' He turned to Zeek. 'We'll have to finish this later.'

Zeek shrugged as if he hadn't a care in the world and walked out of the office with a lolloping gait.

Within seconds of Zeek leaving, Riley Smalls entered

the room. From his general mood he seemed as pleased to see the Mayor as the Mayor was to see him.

'You called for me?' said Smalls, taking a seat opposite the Mayor's desk without being asked if he'd like one.

'Well yes, quite, er, yes,' said Mr Sedgefield, returning to his own seat and offering the television presenter an insincere smile.

'What about?' asked Smalls.

'Well,' said the Mayor, a little awkwardly. 'It's about these programmes of yours… About the Flower Show…'

'What about them?'

'Yes… Right… Well… There's a certain consensus… in the Colony Council, I mean… that your programmes are a little… erm… *negative*… about the Newcomers.'

'Too right they are,' said Smalls, folding his arms with a sanctimonious nod.

'Yes,' said Mr Sedgefield, the corners of his smile beginning to strain. 'And, um, obviously you're entitled to your opinion, but… er… some people can't help but feel that perhaps it would project a better… um… image of the colony, as a… as a… as a whole, you understand, if we were to be a little more… er, what's the word I'm looking for… *positive* about our guests? While they're here? I mean… Your show is broadcast on all public screens and… er… the guests can see the screens and… er… hear what you're saying about them. So *some people* have said that, er…'

'Some people?' queried Smalls, now leaning forward, a little closer to the Mayor. 'You mean you?'

'Well,' said the Mayor, laughing nervously, 'I didn't, I mean, that's to say I, er…'

'Load of nonsense. All a load of nonsense. I didn't ask for any Newcomers. And I've spoken to quite a few people on the Colony Council and they didn't ask for any either. There are questions that need answering, Mr Sedgefield.'

The Mayor shifted awkwardly in his seat, his bottom inadvertently squeaking against the leather upholstery.

'Such as?'

'What's to stop them staying?' demanded Smalls. 'Once this Flower Show's over, I mean. What's to stop all these Newcomers with their fancy clothes and their strange hair staying here on Chelsea 426? There's more than fifty ships' worth of them now, Mr Sedgefield. There's almost as many of them as there are of us. It would only take a few ships' worth of Newcomers to stay and within five years you wouldn't recognise the place. They'd be running in the council elections and then, next thing you know, we'd be amending the Colony Code.'

'Well, now, I don't think we need to worry about *that*,' Mr Sedgefield blustered. 'I mean, *really*…'

'Oh, don't you now?' said Smalls. 'You might not *think* we need to worry, but a lot of people *are* worrying, Mr Sedgefield. A lot of people are. People who vote.'

There was a long pause between the two men. They eyeballed one another across the desk, and the Mayor put his hands together in the shape of a church, the steeple of his forefingers pressed against his lips. He breathed in sharply and let it out with a long, slow sigh.

'I see,' he said, and then, more confidently, as if it were a speech he had rehearsed, 'Well, obviously, though we acknowledge the… *vibrancy* the Newcomers have brought to Chelsea 426, we will ensure that there are tough regulations in place to prevent our way of life from being altered in any way once the Flower Show is over. The important thing here is harmony, I think you'll agree?'

Smalls nodded, though he still wasn't smiling.

'I agree,' he said. 'We want them off this colony the minute the Flower Show is over. All of them.'

'*All* of them?'

'*All* of them.'

'Right. Yes. Of course. Though, actually, that may be a little—'

'I said all of them, Mr Sedgefield,' said Smalls, standing abruptly and straightening his jacket. 'There'll be trouble otherwise. Newcomers getting up to all sorts. Rioting in the streets. And come election time…'

'Yes?'

'Well… Let's just say the people of Chelsea 426 might want the kind of person as Mayor who warned them about this in the first place.'

'You're not saying…?'

'Now, Mr Sedgefield, I'm not an ambitious man, but if civic duty calls… Well, who's to say what tomorrow brings? I trust I'm making myself clear…'

The Mayor nodded sheepishly.

'Crystal,' he replied.

FOUR

Above the entrance to the Oxygen Gardens was an enormous sign:

CHELSEA 426 WELCOMES YOU TO
THE CHELSEA FLOWER SHOW!

The Doctor read the sign. There was something so formal about the way it was written, right down to the choice of font, that it didn't seem particularly welcoming.

Taking off his glasses, the Doctor moved towards the entrance, where a large, almost rectangular security guard stood motionless, his arms at his sides. Even when the Doctor was only a few paces away from him, the guard failed to acknowledge his presence, staring blankly ahead like a waxwork dummy.

The Doctor waited for a response, but none came.

'Hello!' he said eventually.

The guard turned his head and looked down at the Doctor, huffing through his nostrils as if the Doctor's presence alone was enough to ruin his evening.

'Can I help you?' he grunted.

'Well yes, actually,' said the Doctor. 'I was wondering if I could see Professor Wilberforce.'

'Professor Wilberforce?'

'That's right!' said the Doctor, producing a flat leather wallet from his pocket, which he opened and held up for the guard to see. The guard inspected what to him looked like an identity card but was, in fact, a blank piece of psychic paper.

'I'm Doctor John Smith from the Intergalactic Horticultural Society,' said the Doctor, flapping the wallet shut. 'Just thought I'd pop in. Say hello.'

'Right…' said the guard, a little cautiously. 'I'll just radio him and see if he's available.'

'Splendid!' said the Doctor.

The guard spoke through a small walkie-talkie to somebody inside the Oxygen Gardens, and a tinny, barely audible voice answered from the other end of the line.

'If you could just wait here one moment, sir,' said the guard.

'Of course,' said the Doctor.

Before long, a small, prim young woman in wire-framed glasses came out of the Oxygen Gardens and shook the Doctor's hand.

'Doctor Smith,' she said, smiling graciously. 'I'm Alice Wendell. I'm Professor Wilberforce's assistant. Can I help you at all?'

'Oh, hello!' said the Doctor, holding up the wallet once more. 'I'm Doctor Smith, from the Intergalactic Horticultural Society.'

'Yes,' said Alice Wendell. 'So Bruno here tells me.'

'Of course,' said the Doctor. 'Anyway... I was in the neighbourhood and thought I'd pop by and say hello to old Professor Wilberforce. See how he is, you know?'

'Well I'm afraid Professor Wilberforce is very busy right now,' said Alice, 'as I'm sure you'll appreciate. We have less than sixteen hours until the opening of the Flower Show.'

'Of course...'

'Will you be attending tomorrow?'

The Doctor nodded thoughtfully.

'Hopefully, yes...'

'You aren't *from* Chelsea 426, are you?'

The Doctor stopped nodding and looked straight at Alice, raising both eyebrows.

'I'm sorry, what's that?'

'I said you aren't *from* Chelsea 426. Are you?'

'Oh no... No no no no no... Just visiting.'

'Just visiting,' said Alice, 'and yet you are only *hoping* to visit the Flower Show?'

The Doctor raised one index finger to his lip and nodded thoughtfully.

'Right, yeah, well, that's if I can get a ticket,' he said. 'I was kind of hoping I might get a sneak preview. Being from the Intergalactic Horticultural Society and everything.'

'I'm afraid that will not be agreeable.' Alice smiled politely. 'We have many visitors from many worlds. We're unable to offer… *sneak previews*… to anyone. You'll just have to wait for the show like everybody else.'

'Of course. Yes. Silly me.'

'Good evening, Doctor Smith.'

'Oh,' said the Doctor.

The guard had stepped forward from his post so that he stood between the Doctor and Alice, an unspoken indication for the Doctor to leave.

'Right, yes. I see. Well, I suppose I'll just have to come back tomorrow, then.'

'Yes,' said Alice. '*If* you can get a ticket, of course.'

'Right, of course,' said the Doctor. 'I'll get onto it straight away. Get my people to phone your people.'

And with that he about-turned and walked casually away from them, looking back over his shoulder just once to meet their icy glares. When he was out of their sight he opened the wallet of psychic paper once more and ran one finger over the blank page.

'She didn't buy you for a second, did she?' he said, snapping it shut and walking away.

Professor Wilberforce stood in one corner of his office, his hand laid flat on the top of the glass dome containing the single blue flower.

'Soon,' he purred softly. 'Soon…'

He heard the door to his study open and turned to face Alice. Nodding without saying a word, he sat behind his desk, bathed in the dim, multicoloured light from his Tiffany lamp.

'Were you listening?' Alice asked.

The Professor shook his head.

'Our thoughts aren't strong enough yet,' he said. 'These human brains are weak. But give it time. Who was it?'

'He called himself Doctor Smith,' said Alice. 'He tried to use psychic paper to confirm his credentials.'

Professor Wilberforce laughed and shook his head.

'The fool,' he said. 'He claimed to be a *doctor*?'

'Yes,' said Alice.

Professor Wilberforce nodded thoughtfully, and then pressed a small brass button on the edge of his desk. A thin, transparent glass screen rose up from its surface. As the screen flickered into life it revealed an image of Mr Pemberton, the shopkeeper.

'We have had a visitor,' said Professor Wilberforce. 'A Newcomer.'

'So have we,' said Mr Pemberton. 'He came here with the Carstairs twins, the little blighters.'

Professor Wilberforce nodded.

'And how did your visitor refer to himself?' he asked, leaning in close to the screen. 'When he came to your shop, what did he call himself?'

'He called himself the Doctor,' said Mr Pemberton.

'Oh really?' said Professor Wilberforce, smiling now, his hands clasped together with his forefingers braced against his chin. 'How very interesting.'

It was night-time, or at least, under a sky that was forever black and speckled with stars, it was an hour that meant it was night.

The Doctor sat at the bar of the Grand Hotel, quietly nursing a glass of orange juice.

Beside him sat an old man with a white handlebar moustache, dressed in a tweed suit and waistcoat, and sipping a large glass of cognac.

'Of course,' said the old man in a gruff, clipped English accent, 'talk to the young 'uns today and they won't believe you. They weren't there. The Battle of Olympus Mons. Saw 'em coming over the ridge, you know, like a million little spiders, armed to the teeth.'

He lifted up his arms, miming the action of aiming and firing a rifle.

'Bang!' he shouted. 'Bang bang! Four of 'em... five of 'em... blew one fella's chin off. And then, out of the sky…' He looked up at the ceiling, feigning surprise, waving his hands in mock horror.

'Aaagh!' he yelled. 'And they swooped down, like flying monkeys, you know? Caw caw! Caw caw!'

Standing behind the bar, drying a glass with a tea towel, Mr Carstairs shook his head.

'Is the Major bothering you?'

'No,' said the Doctor, smiling. 'Not at all.'

'Nother one, Mr Carstairs, if you'd be so kind,' interrupted the Major, taking a hefty swig from his glass and then holding it up.

As Mr Carstairs poured the Major another drink, the old man turned to the Doctor and held out his hand.

'I'm frightfully sorry, old chap,' he said, his moustache twitching from side to side as he spoke, 'but I didn't quite catch your name.'

'I'm the Doctor,' said the Doctor, shaking his hand. 'And you're the Major?'

The Major nodded.

'Yes,' he said. Then he leaned in close and spoke in hushed tones. 'Though I'm not actually a major, you know.'

'Really?' said the Doctor, smiling. 'Well there's a coincidence.'

Mr Carstairs gave the Major his brandy and then cast his gaze on the Doctor. The Doctor could still sense the hotel owner's evident distrust.

'So, Doctor,' said Mr Carstairs, eventually. 'Will you

be visiting the Flower Show tomorrow?'

The Doctor tilted his head from side to side, as if mulling it over.

'Possibly,' he said, and then, 'Depends if I can get a ticket. Yourself?'

'Oh, no,' said Mr Carstairs. 'We're much too busy for that.'

The Doctor looked around the bar, which was empty but for himself, the Major and Mr Carstairs.

'Really?' he said. '*Really*? Seems awfully quiet. Considering the Flower Show starts tomorrow, I mean.'

Mr Carstairs' eyes met the Doctor's and he offered a curt nod.

'Yes, well,' he said. 'Business has been a little slower than anticipated, but I'm sure all that will change.'

The Doctor nodded, taking a sip of his drink.

'I must say, though,' he said, 'I'm a little bit curious about what brought you and Mrs Carstairs here in the first place.'

Mr Carstairs shook his head as if the question were an affront, laughing nervously.

'You're very forward with your questions, aren't you?' he said.

'Sorry if I'm being nosey,' said the Doctor. 'It's just Earth, right now... The beginning of the twenty-sixth century... They'd be about due for the Third Renaissance, if I'm not mistaken. The Theatre of Nomogan? The ceilings of the Chamber of Ra? The Simarine Orchestra? I mean… Everyone's talking about those things, and they'll be talking about them for centuries, and yet here you are… Out here… On Chelsea 426.'

'Yes,' said Mr Carstairs. 'Earth is certainly very cosmopolitan. A little *too* cosmopolitan, if you know what I mean.'

The Doctor's smile faded. He understood all too well what that meant.

'Right,' he said, getting up off his stool. 'Well… I really should be hitting the old dusty trail. There's all the excitement of the Flower Show to look forward to tomorrow.'

'Quite,' said Mr Carstairs, forcing a curt smile. 'Goodnight, Doctor.'

'Goodnight.'

'Yes… G'night!' slurred the Major. 'Always sleep with a pistol under me pillow, you know. Never know when the swine are gonna cut your throat in the night, what!'

'Goodnight, Major,' said the Doctor, smiling once more.

As the Doctor left the bar the Major lifted his glass to his lips and took another swig.

'Same old Grand Hotel,' he said. 'People come, people go. Nothing ever happens.'

'Mr Pemberton,' said Wallace, as he and Mr Pemberton approached the entrance of the Oxygen Gardens, 'are you sure this is all right? With Professor Wilberforce, I mean? There's people paying good money for tickets to see the Flower Show.'

'Of course it is, lad, of course it is,' said Mr Pemberton. 'I managed to get my hands on a dozen new thermometers for him only last month. He asked if there was any way he could repay the favour, after paying us good money, of course, and I said I wouldn't mind taking a look at the show when there's not Newcomers cluttering up the place and making it look untidy.'

'Oh, right.'

'And I said, "Mind if I bring the lad along?" and he said, "Not at all." So here we are.'

When they reached the entrance, the guard there nodded to Mr Pemberton and spoke into his walkie-talkie. Moments later Professor Wilberforce was there to greet them.

'Ah, Mr Pemberton!' said Wilberforce. 'And this must be Wallace. Come on in. Everything's ready for tomorrow morning. The *Caeruliflora Saturnalis* is looking particularly resplendent this evening, I must say.'

Wallace and Mr Pemberton followed the Professor into the Oxygen Gardens, down a dark and narrow metal corridor and out into the main chamber itself.

Wallace failed to suppress a gasp upon seeing the scale of the plants there. When he'd heard all the talk of the Flower Show, he had imagined pretty little things like his mother grew in pots around the house, not the gigantic creation that towered over them now.

'Well,' said Professor Wilberforce, beaming down at Wallace, 'what do you think?'

'Yes, sir,' said Wallace, nodding enthusiastically. 'Very impressive, sir.'

'As you can see,' Wilberforce continued, 'they come in all shapes and sizes, from our biggest specimen all the way down to the smaller shrubs here.'

He gestured towards a flowerbed lined from front to back with rows of similarly exotic blue flowers.

'They have an exquisite perfume,' said Professor Wilberforce. 'Perhaps you would care to sample it?'

Wallace looked from the Professor to Mr Pemberton and frowned.

'Go and smell it, boy,' said Mr Pemberton.

Wallace nodded nervously, and stepped a little closer to the flowerbed. He leaned over its outer edge towards one of the flowers, and breathed in. He wasn't really sure what the Professor was talking about; he couldn't smell a thing.

'Lean a little closer, Wallace,' said Professor Wilberforce, 'and breathe in slowly. Take the perfume in and savour it, my boy.'

Wallace did as the Professor said, but this time, as he breathed in, the flower shook violently and emitted a fine green cloud of dust. Wallace coughed and gagged, and stumbled back, away from the flowerbed, before falling to the ground with a thud.

As he writhed in agony at their feet, Professor Wilberforce and Mr Pemberton smiled down at him.

'There there,' said Mr Pemberton. 'It'll all be over in a moment.'

Back in his room at the Grand Hotel, the Doctor paced back and forth, occasionally standing at the window to look down at the western edges of the colony. He'd only ever visited Saturn on a handful of occasions, primarily because there wasn't a great deal to visit in the first place, but the one thing that never failed to impress was the horizon. On most worlds, there is a slight and almost imperceptible curve to the horizon. It's so slight most creatures don't even notice it, but it's there. Saturn was so vast a planet that no such curvature was noticeable, not even to a Time Lord. It genuinely seemed as if the world were flat.

The only feature out there on the blank and boundless canvas of Saturn's surface was the storm they called the Great White Spot. From this height it was almost flat, an enormous grey disc sweeping inwards with monstrous grace towards a dark vortex. More dramatic than the unending flatness of the horizon or even the Great White Spot was the appearance, to the south, of Saturn's rings. They arced up from where the planet's flesh-coloured clouds met the black infinity of space, like the blade of an impossibly large scimitar, before tapering away into the darkness.

The Doctor would have found it all indescribably beautiful if he hadn't been quite so concerned.

Something wasn't right on Chelsea 426, though he couldn't say for certain what it was. The only thing he knew for sure was that he was going to find out.

FIVE

Where's Jake? thought Vienna, as she polished the last of the dining room tables. They had agreed to meet in the dining room to finish their chores before breakfast, but he still wasn't there.

Vienna could only imagine that he was still snoring under his duvet, while she was here, scrubbing and polishing. When the doors at the far end of the dining room opened, she hoped it might be her brother, still a little bit sleepy but ready to help finish the task. To her disappointment, it was their mother.

'There's somebody here to see you,' said Mrs Carstairs, icily. 'That boy from the hardware shop.'

'Wallace?' asked Vienna, smiling and then composing herself, not wanting her mother to sense enthusiasm.

'Yes, I think that's his name,' said Mrs Carstairs, holding the door open as Vienna ran through.

Her pace slowed to a walk as she neared the lobby. Wallace was waiting for her at the reception desk, shifting awkwardly from foot to foot, his shoulders slumped, holding an envelope in both hands.

'Morning, Vienna,' he said, looking up at her bashfully.

'Morning, Wallace,' said Vienna. 'You wanted to see me?'

Wallace nodded. 'Yeah,' he said, holding out the envelope. 'I just wanted to give you these.'

Vienna took the envelope from him and tore it open in an instant. She reached inside with her forefinger and thumb and pulled out four shiny tickets.

'The Flower Show?' she asked, her face lighting up with glee. '*Four* tickets to the Flower Show?'

Wallace nodded before averting his gaze once more to the tiled floor.

'Oh, wow!' said Vienna. 'But how did you… I mean, these must have cost a fortune!'

'Mr Pemberton won them,' said Wallace. 'In a raffle.'

'A raffle? But I didn't hear about any raffle.'

'Yeah… It was the shopkeepers. They… they had a raffle.'

Mrs Carstairs appeared at Vienna's side and looked down at the tickets in her daughter's hand.

'What are those?' she asked.

'Tickets to the Flower Show!' said Vienna. 'Mr Pemberton won them in a raffle. He gave them to Wallace, and Wallace has given them to me!'

'Really?' said Mrs Carstairs, unimpressed. 'And why doesn't Mr Pemberton want them?'

Wallace looked up at Mrs Carstairs very suddenly, with a mean look in his eyes that took the woman by surprise. He'd always seemed like such a shy and nervous boy, but that look, that penetrating gaze, chilled her blood.

Wallace's expression softened, and was replaced with a crooked smile.

'He's already got some. And I'm going with my mum next week, so I thought you might want them.'

'Well,' said Mrs Carstairs, still a little shaken, 'that's… that's very kind of you, Wallace. Thank the boy, Vienna.'

'Thank you!' said Vienna, beaming,

'Anyways,' said Wallace, biting his lower lip, 'I'd best be going. Lots to do at the shop.'

He looked at Mrs Carstairs once more and flashed a smile that she still found strangely hard and menacing.

'Thank you, Wallace,' she said uneasily. 'This is very generous of you.'

'Don't mention it.'

'And thank Mr Pemberton for us,' added Mrs Carstairs.

'Oh, I will,' said Wallace, still smiling as he made his way towards the hotel's exit.

'Wallace!' called Vienna.

He turned to face her.

'Maybe I'll see you later?'

'Yes,' said Wallace. 'That would be agreeable.'

And with that he left the hotel, turning back to look at her just once as he made his way down Tunbridge Street.

'Hmm,' said Mrs Carstairs, disapprovingly. 'Tickets to the Flower Show, indeed. Probably stole them.'

Vienna looked at her mother with an angry frown.

'When was the last time anyone stole anything here?' she snapped.

'Vienna Carstairs, I will thank you kindly not to use that tone of voice with me, young girl. It's the Newcomers. They come here and they bring their Earth ways with them. Just you mark my words.'

Vienna sulked and looked back down at the tickets.

'So when are we going to the Flower Show?' she asked.

'Well, your father and I can't go,' said Mrs Carstairs. 'We're far too busy with things here.'

From behind the reception desk, Mr Carstairs emerged from his office.

'Finished polishing those tables, have we?' he asked, somewhat sarcastically.

'Almost,' replied Vienna.

'Oh, I see,' said Mr Carstairs. 'So that would explain all this standing around in the lobby partaking in idle chit-chat. What have you got there, anyway?'

Vienna held up the tickets for him to see and smiled again.

'Tickets to the Flower Show! Four of them!' she said. 'Wallace, Mr Pemberton's assistant, he brought them round.'

Mrs Carstairs turned to her husband.

'Won them in a raffle, apparently,' she said, pursing her lips. 'I've told Vienna there's no question of us going. We're far too busy.'

Mr Carstairs looked at the tickets, at his daughter's smile, and then at his wife.

'Nonsense,' he said, allowing a faint smile of his own to lift the corners of his mouth. 'We only need one of us to stay here. It's not *that* busy. How about you and the twins go down there and take a look at it. Won't do any harm you leaving the hotel for an hour or two. I hardly think we're going to be inundated with guests in your absence, dear.'

Mrs Carstairs shook her head impatiently and looked at the tickets. She rolled her eyes and shook her head again.

'Oh, all right then,' she said, finally giving in. 'But only for an hour. I'm not wasting my time looking at a lot of silly old flowers while there's work to be done.'

Mr Carstairs turned to Vienna and winked, and

Vienna let out a little squeal of excitement which she muted very quickly.

'Talking of work,' said Mrs Carstairs, 'where's that brother of yours?'

The *Pride of Deimos* was, quite possibly, the most famous leisure ship in the galaxy.

A mile long, its hull as reflective as polished chrome, its solar sails like the wings of a colossal butterfly, there was hardly a person alive who hadn't heard its name, which was synonymous with wealth and luxury. The *Pride of Deimos*. And there it was, gliding in towards Chelsea 426.

Jake watched as it passed by the viewing windows of room 237, hardly daring to breathe. On its deck he saw dozens, perhaps hundreds of guests, standing under the shimmering blue haze of the force fields. The men were dressed in dinner jackets and bow ties, the women in ball gowns; the kind of people Jake had only ever seen in photographs and films. The *Pride of Deimos* was a very different place to the colony he thought of as home.

When the ship had finally passed, banking sharply at the south west corner of the colony, Jake sighed and stepped down from the window, making sure to wipe away his fingerprints from the glass. He picked up his dog-eared copy of *Cowley's Almanac of Spacecraft* and gazed down at the picture that filled almost two whole pages: a panoramic photograph of the *Pride of Deimos*.

He'd seen that picture countless times, and read every single bit of information about the ship. He knew its length and breadth, the size of its engines and the maximum number of crew and passengers it could hold. *Cowley's Almanac* was the most cherished book in his small collection, hence its curled corners and its creased spine, and he had read every entry, time and time again. Closing the book and tucking it into the back pocket of his jeans he tiptoed out of Room 237, checking that the coast was clear before stepping into the corridor.

He closed the door as quietly as he could, but was no more than five steps away from it when a voice behind him said, 'She really is quite a beauty, isn't she?'

He turned to see the Doctor.

'I'm sorry…?' he asked.

'The *Pride of Deimos*,' said the Doctor. 'Quite impressive. If you like that sort of thing. Me… I've always preferred a bit of mess. Never could get used to the whole five-star thing. Far too posh for me.'

'Oh, yeah, right,' said Jake.

Together, Jake and the Doctor took the elevator down to the lobby. As they stepped out through the doors they were greeted by an angry-looking Mr and Mrs Carstairs.

'And what time do you call this?' asked Jake's father. 'Your sister's just about finished polishing those tables. By herself, might I add.'

'Sorry, Dad,' said Jake. 'Slept late.'

Before Mr Carstairs could scold his son any further, Vienna walked out into the lobby.

'All done!' she said, and then, turning to her brother, 'No thanks to you!'

'I said I'm sorry…' said Jake sulkily.

'Anyway,' said Vienna, 'can we go now? Can we? Can we?'

'Well I suppose so,' said Mrs Carstairs.

'Going anywhere nice?' asked the Doctor.

'We're going to the Flower Show!' said Vienna. 'Wallace gave us tickets! You too, Jake!'

'Oh, whoop-di-doo,' said Jake.

'So you don't want to go, then?'

'I didn't say *that*, did I?'

'Anyway,' said Vienna, now turning to the Doctor, 'we've got a spare ticket because Dad can't come. Did you want it?'

Mrs Carstairs pursed her lips and snapped her head in Vienna's direction, but her daughter paid her no attention.

'A spare ticket, you say?' replied the Doctor.

Vienna nodded enthusiastically.

'Yeah,' she said. 'So are you coming, or what?'

The Doctor looked to Jake, who was grinning from ear to ear, and then to Mrs Carstairs, who had folded her arms.

'What do *you* say, Mrs C?' he asked.

'Well,' said Mrs Carstairs, through gritted teeth, 'I suppose it would only go to waste otherwise.'

'I guess that means I'm coming,' said the Doctor.

Huffing through flared nostrils and shaking her head, Mrs Carstairs led her children out onto Tunbridge Street, and the Doctor followed.

SIX

'Tickets, please,' said the usher.

Vienna passed the tickets on to her mother, who in turn handed them over. The tickets were torn and the stubs handed back to Mrs Carstairs, and then the four of them filed through the arched entrance to the Oxygen Gardens.

Jake looked back over his shoulder to see that the Doctor was now wearing a pair of black-framed spectacles. He seemed to be inspecting almost every detail of the corridor, as if each pipe and valve was endlessly fascinating. As they neared the main chamber, the Doctor paused momentarily and began sniffing the air.

'What is it?' asked Jake.

'Oh, nothing,' said the Doctor. 'Probably nothing. *Hopefully* nothing.'

'This way, please,' said a second usher, walking backwards with his hands held up, beckoning the guests forward.

Jake had never seen so many Newcomers before, so many different faces. In the two years that his family had lived on Chelsea 426, he had become used to seeing the same people, day after day. Even if he couldn't put a name to every face, he did, at least, recognise almost everyone he saw on a daily basis. There were occasional visitors, from time to time – traders mostly, or those who were passing through and stopping to refuel or rest before embarking on a longer journey – but they were never this great in number. Looking around at the slowly shuffling army of guests, Jake realised he saw very few faces he knew at all.

In the main chamber of the Oxygen Gardens, the guests were guided into place in the walkways and thoroughfares beneath the colossal glass dome. To either side, large sections of the chamber were hidden from view by curtains suspended from the dome itself. No flowers or plants were yet visible. On the far side of the gardens a small stage had been set up on which there stood a lectern and a microphone, and behind the stage two large video screens and a sign announcing the 'First Ever Chelsea Flower Show'.

There was then a long and tiresome wait, as the

last of the guests came through the doors, and the whole chamber echoed with an increasingly excitable chattering. Young waiters and waitresses passed among them carrying trays filled with glasses of champagne or orange juice. Jake surreptitiously reached for a flute of champagne, but felt his mother's disapproving glare and chose an orange juice instead.

While Mrs Carstairs shifted restlessly and impatiently, and his sister went up on tiptoes to get a better view, Jake noticed that the Doctor seemed anxious, eagerly trying to look behind the curtains. He was still sniffing at the air as if he could smell something distinctly unpleasant; his expression not one of excitement or enthusiasm, like the guests, nor one of quiet irritation, like his mother, but of concern. The Doctor looked like he was intensely worried about something. But what?

'What is it?' Jake asked eventually. 'What's the matter?'

'Oh, nothing,' said the Doctor. 'Just… I don't know… A hunch.'

The Doctor raised one hand and, deep in thought, tapped out a silent Morse code on his lips with his forefinger. Then he leaned forward and said to Jake, as quietly as he could, 'If I give you the signal, I want you to get your mother and sister out of here as soon as you can.'

Jake's eyes opened a little wider.

'What signal?'

The Doctor nodded thoughtfully.

'I'll shout, "Now!" The word "Now". How does that sound?'

Jake snorted and shook his head.

'Not much of a secret signal,' he said.

'It won't have to be a secret,' said the Doctor.

'What are you worried about?'

'Oh, I don't know, it might be nothing,' replied the Doctor. 'Probably just me, worrying about noth—'

Before he could end his sentence, the whole chamber echoed with the loud thudding of Professor Wilberforce tapping at his microphone. The chattering of the guests stopped abruptly, and everyone in the gardens turned to face the stage and the Professor.

'Thank you, thank you,' said Professor Wilberforce. 'Ladies and gentlemen… Residents of Chelsea 426 and our esteemed guests from across the cosmos, may I take this opportunity to welcome you to this, the first ever Chelsea Flower Show.'

The guests began to clap. Jake eventually joined in, but he noticed that the Doctor wasn't paying any attention, looking this way and that at everything except the stage.

'When I was studying as a botanist on Earth,' Wilberforce continued, 'I was informed, by my tutors, that Earth was the only body in our solar system capable of supporting plant life. Almost thirty-five years later we, here on Chelsea 426, have proven them wrong.'

Behind the Professor, the two video screens came alive, showing images of Saturn and the eddying clouds of its surface.

'In my time here at the colony it has been a rudimentary practice for us to take samples from the planet's atmosphere, something we carry out, without fail, on a weekly basis. It has enabled us to develop a greater understanding of the planet we now call home, but more importantly it allows us to sleep safely in the knowledge that this colony and the planet itself enjoy a harmonious relationship, each kept in careful balance by the maintenance of the fusion candle and the tiniest of adjustments to our flotation panels…'

Jake looked up at the Doctor, feigning a yawn, but the Doctor still wasn't paying any attention to him *or* the Professor's speech.

'For almost two decades, this practice had proven quite uneventful. Saturn is a relatively stable world with little in the way of surprises. Or so we thought. A little over a year ago, we came upon what can only be described as a vast cloud of microscopic spores buried a little over sixty kilometres beneath the outer layers of the planet's atmosphere. The cloud itself was vast, large enough to block out the sun over the entire continent of Africa…'

The audience gasped.

'Though of course,' said Professor Wilberforce, laughing softly, 'on a planet that is itself so many times the size of Earth, this is comparatively small. We took samples from the cloud and, bringing them back to the colony, found they were, in fact, biological matter. After many experiments, we learned that these spores were very similar to those one might find on Earth, and so we provided them with a nurturing environment. The results were astounding… As I'm sure you'll agree.'

Professor Wilberforce opened his arms wide in a grand gesture, and all around the gardens the curtains began rising up towards the ceiling of the dome, revealing dozens of square and rectangular flowerbeds, each one filled with outlandish-looking flowers and broad-leaved plants. The audience gasped as one, and the garden was filled with an almost deafening chatter.

'Ladies and gentlemen,' said Professor Wilberforce, 'I give you – the plant life of Saturn!'

The audience began to applaud, first clapping and then whooping and cheering. Jake saw his mother clapping politely, but she was sincerely unimpressed by the more vocal enthusiasm of the Newcomers. The Doctor, meanwhile, was gazing up at the colossal blue flower in the centre of the chamber, a monstrous thing that very nearly touched the ceiling.

'But,' he said, 'but… that's *impossible*…'

'Why?' Jake asked over the din of the guests.

'Well,' said the Doctor, 'there *aren't* any plants on Saturn.'

Jake looked at him with a dismissive sneer.

'How would you know?' he asked. 'I mean... Look around you. What are *these*?'

Jake followed the Doctor's gaze up the thick and slimy green trunk of the largest plant, toward the flower at its crest.

Was he mistaken, or was it actually moving? There was no breeze, no wind, but it looked as if it was swaying.

No, not swaying. The trunk of the plant was writhing, the flowered head tilting forward. If Jake hadn't known better, he would have thought that the flower was staring straight at them.

And still, the crowd applauded.

'Oh, this isn't good...' said the Doctor, and then, shouting as loud as he could, 'Everybody out! Now!'

'Doctor?' snapped Mrs Carstairs. 'Have you gone mad?'

People were now staring at the Doctor with quizzical frowns, but none of them were moving.

'Sorry, are you all hard of hearing?' said the Doctor. 'I said everybody leave! *Now!*'

Heads turned, and some people began muttering to one another, but soon enough their voices were drowned out as the largest of the plants let out a deafening noise, like a cacophonous belch. From its bulbous blue flower, it released a massive cloud of dust which descended onto the gardens like a thick green fog.

All at once the gardens fell into an eerie silence,

and then, as the first guests began to inhale the vile green dust, that silence was replaced by coughing and spluttering.

'Come on!' shouted the Doctor. 'What are you all waiting for? Mrs Carstairs… we have to go!'

Clutching Jake and Vienna by their arms the Doctor made a bolt for the exits.

Jake looked back to see his mother frozen to the spot, her face a mask of shock as those around her collapsed to the ground, clutching at their throats.

'Mum!' he shouted, a single tear streaming down his cheek. 'Mum!'

His mother shook her head, the colour draining from her cheeks, and then began to follow them, nearly tripping over fallen bodies as she did. With the Doctor now dragging both Jake and Vienna out into the corridor, Jake saw his mother gasping for air in the last few seconds before she too collapsed, disappearing from view.

As guests and residents alike ran screaming out of the Oxygen Gardens, the Doctor took Jake and Vienna as far as the garden's entrance and then stopped.

'Right,' he said. 'Wait here.'

'Where are you going?' asked Vienna. 'Where's Mum?'

'Just wait here,' said the Doctor once more, before turning sharply on his heels and then swimming against the tide of fleeing guests.

Vienna turned to her brother. 'What's happening?' she asked, tears welling in her eyes.

'I don't know,' said Jake. 'I just don't know…'

More and more people came flooding out of the exits, many of them dazed and ashen-faced, and then there were no more. The sliding doors slid shut with a mechanical hiss, and Jake and Vienna were alone.

'Where *is* he?' asked Vienna, but her brother could only shake his head.

They waited for seconds that felt like hours, neither of them daring to breathe, then suddenly the doors whooshed open once more, and the Doctor came running out with Mrs Carstairs on his shoulder.

'Right!' he said, breathing out as if he been holding his breath underwater. 'That wasn't as easy as I thought it would be. Let's go!'

The Major sat in an armchair in the lobby of the Grand Hotel, a copy of the *Chelsea Bugle* open in his lap. He'd been reading it only a minute or so, grunting occasionally in displeasure, or huffing in agreement, before he folded it noisily and turned his attention to Mr Carstairs.

'Of course,' he said, 'back in '58 we were stuck in the swamps for a fortnight. Ten of us clinging to a raft like limpets. Flinty bought it when a dragonfly the size of an albatross came down. Bit his head clean off.'

'Really, Major?' said Mr Carstairs, making no attempt to sound even vaguely interested.

'Oh yes,' said the Major. 'And the leeches there were the size of bananas. Course, bit of hairspray and a naked flame soon saw to those nasty little beggars. Tough thing to come by on the moons of Mercutio 14, mind, hairspray. Luckily Migs had a tin going spare, or we'd have been sucked dry.'

Before the Major could continue his story, the lobby doors hissed open and Jake and Vienna came running into the hotel, out of breath and white with fear.

'What's the matter?' said Mr Carstairs. 'What's all the commotion?'

Seconds later, the Doctor ran into the lobby, still carrying Mrs Carstairs.

'Good grief!' said Mr Carstairs. 'What have you done to her?'

The Doctor lowered her into the armchair next to the Major, and paused to catch his breath.

'Blimey!' said the Major. 'Looks like Mrs C's caught a nasty case of drixoid fever, what? Only thing for it is a pint and a half of cod liver oil, straight down in one go.'

'It's the Flower Show,' said the Doctor. 'Something's happened. We need to get your wife upstairs.'

Mr Carstairs was now out from behind the reception desk and crouched beside his wife, who remained unconscious. The twins stood away from them, holding each other and crying.

'You say something happened,' snapped Mr Carstairs. '*What* happened?'

'It was the flowers,' said the Doctor. 'They let out this… this green gas. We need to take your wife to my room.'

'Your room? Why on Earth would we need to do that?'

'Well,' said the Doctor, 'firstly, we're not on Earth, and secondly, I'm a doctor. No, not just *a* doctor, I'm *the* Doctor. Just trust me on this.'

Together, Mr Carstairs and the Doctor carried Mrs Carstairs to the elevator, the children following closely behind, leaving just the Major in the lobby.

'I guess I'll hold the fort then,' he said, getting to his feet. 'This reminds me of the Siege of the Hexion Gates…'

'What *is* that?' said Mr Carstairs, lowering his wife carefully onto the bed. The children stood beside him, equally dumbfounded.

'It's a TARDIS,' said the Doctor.

'I'm sorry,' said Mr Carstairs, 'but would you mind speaking in English?'

'It's a kind of spaceship,' the Doctor replied. 'It's *my* spaceship.'

'But how did you get it here?' asked Vienna. 'In your *room*? It's *bigger than the door.*'

'Yes, well… Long story short and all the rest of it… I didn't push it through the door. I just… kind of… well, parked it here, really.'

'This is madness,' said Mr Carstairs. 'First you talk of plants attacking my wife and now you *park* a spaceship in your room? Tell me, Doctor Smith—'

'Actually, just "Doctor" is fine.'

'Tell me, *Doctor*… How do we know that you aren't involved in all these goings on?'

'Just trust me,' said the Doctor. 'I'm not. Now you take care of Mrs Carstairs. I won't be a mo.'

And with that the Doctor opened a door in the blue box and stepped inside. Through the narrow opening in the door, Jake, Vienna and their father heard the clanking of footsteps, and then a series of banging and crashing sounds.

'Oh, where *is it*?' the Doctor shouted, his voice echoing around what sounded like a cave.

Jake walked gingerly towards the TARDIS.

'Jake, please don't do that,' said his father, but Jake continued until he had reached the door.

Gently, he pushed it open until the gap was wide enough to lean in, and poked his head inside.

'Oh…' he said, laughing in disbelief, his voice resounding around the interior of the blue box. 'Oh, you would not *believe* this…'

'What is it?' asked Vienna, running across the room to join him.

Standing at her brother's side she pulled him out of the doorway and leaned through herself.

'But…' she said, stepping backwards and pulling the

door back to where it had been, 'but… but… I mean… That's… It can't…'

Seconds later the Doctor emerged from the TARDIS once more, holding what looked like a very small, thin telescope with a suction cup at one end.

'Doctor,' said Jake, pulling at his sleeve as he crossed the room to where their mother lay, 'Doctor, your ship… We just… Your ship… It's… I mean, it's…'

'I know,' said the Doctor, crouching now beside Mrs Carstairs.

He placed the suction cup end of the device to his right eye and flicked a switch. Suddenly, there appeared at the other end of the miniature telescope a pencil-thin beam of green light which the Doctor aimed at Mrs Carstairs' nose and mouth.

'Fascinating,' he said. 'This is just fascinating.'

'It may be fascinating to you, Doctor,' said Mr Carstairs, his voice trembling with emotion, 'but this is my *wife*. What's wrong with her?'

'They're spores,' the Doctor said, leaning in closer so that the device was now almost touching her face. 'Tiny little spores. Probably like the ones the plants came from in the first place. I'm just analysing their chemical composition… Just a second…'

There was a long pause, and Jake and Vienna sat beside their father, who without thinking about it put his arms around them and held them close.

'Fascinating,' the Doctor said again. 'There's not

enough chlorophyll for a Derridean Orchid. The carbon levels are too high for a Krynoid. No… This is something else. It's familiar, I'll give it that… But what *is it?*'

With a hacking cough that made everyone except for the Doctor jump, Mrs Carstairs woke very suddenly, and sat bolt upright. She looked around the room; at the Doctor, her husband, and then her children.

'Oh, Bess…' said Mr Carstairs, hugging his wife as hard as he could, but she didn't respond. 'Bess… I thought we'd lost you.'

'I feel unusual,' said Mrs Carstairs.

'That's all right, dear,' replied her husband. 'We'll get you downstairs and make you a nice cup of tea, and then we'll call a doctor.' He shot a resentful glance at the Doctor. 'A *proper* doctor.'

'That would be agreeable,' replied Mrs Carstairs.

'Wait a minute,' said the Doctor, stepping back and switching off the small telescope. 'What did you just say? "That would be agreeable"? Something's not… I mean… Who says that? I mean, OK, I know this place is a bit, well, *weird*, but who says that? *That would be agreeable?*'

'Doctor,' said Mr Carstairs with mounting impatience, 'what *are* you talking about?'

'That shopkeeper, Mr Pemberton, said it yesterday,' said the Doctor. 'And then the assistant, at the botanical centre – she said it last night, or a variation on a theme, anyway. It's like… It's like…' He paced around the room wriggling his fingers in concentration, and then eventually shouted, 'Yes! It's like it's trying to copy human speech but there's one thing it hasn't quite mastered. It's got everything except an affirmative yes or no. It can say yes or no, but when it's trying to qualify the fact it gets it all jumbled up, like its vocabulary is limited or it's making a mistranslation! Yes! I'm brilliant!'

Mrs Carstairs looked blankly at the Doctor, betraying no emotion.

'Doctor,' said Mr Carstairs, 'none of this is making the slightest bit of sense. Now if you don't mind, I'm going to take my wife downstairs and we are going to seek the assistance of a professional we can trust. One who, no offence, *doesn't* spout incomprehensible babble.'

'No,' said the Doctor. 'No no no no no… If I'm right, and trust me, I *am*, this isn't your wife.'

'Doctor, please… I think we've all had enough of this nonsense for one day.'

'No, you see… The spores, from the plant… They're a sentient life form. They—'

'Good day, Doctor.'

Mr Carstairs helped his wife to her feet, walking her out into the corridor, and the children followed. As they were leaving the room, Vienna turned around to face the Doctor.

'Wallace,' she said, tears welling in her eyes. 'Wallace said it to me earlier. When he gave me the tickets. He said, "That would be agreeable".'

'Wallace gave you the tickets?' said the Doctor, and then, remembering that Vienna had already told him this, 'Wallace gave you the tickets! Of course! Right... Vienna, I need you to make sure that your mother doesn't leave the hotel, OK? Just... Just make sure she stays here. And don't go anywhere near any plants. Not unless they're, I don't know, a poinsettia or something.'

He followed them along the corridor and into the elevator, and together they went down to the lobby, Mrs Carstairs never once taking her eyes off the Doctor, though she was still quite expressionless.

It was as they left the elevator and entered the lobby that the Major came running out from behind the desk, his face flushed, pointing towards the upper windows.

'Mr Carstairs, Mr Carstairs!' he cried. 'There appears to be a spot of bother on the bridge.'

Out there, in the black skies above the colony, a ship was coming into view. It was a large craft made of a dark grey metal, a central sphere surrounded by what looked like colossal, spindly claws.

'Oh no,' said the Doctor. 'Not good...'

'What?' asked Jake, anxiously. 'What is it?'

'Sontarans.'

SEVEN

Mayor Sedgefield sat in his office before a bank of monitors and surveyed the chaos outside. From one end of the colony to the other sirens were wailing, which would ordinarily have led to an evacuation, except that all exits had been locked. By whom, he couldn't say. On screen after screen he saw technicians battling to open doors, and failing.

Elsewhere he saw the people of Chelsea 426 running through the narrow streets and across the piazzas and gardens, but running where? There was nowhere to go.

Then he saw them.

They appeared first in the loading bays of the Western Docks: flashes of red and purple light and then – where previously there had been empty space

– soldiers. Dozens if not hundreds of soldiers dressed from head to foot in identical dark blue armour, their heads covered with wide dome-like helmets. Soldiers armed with rifles.

He saw the same flashes of light in other parts of the colony: the Southern Docks, Miramont Gardens. More and more flashes of light and more and more soldiers.

'Mr Mayor,' said a voice on the intercom, stuttering with fear, 'Mr Mayor… There are people on board, sir. They're armed. What should we do?'

Mayor Sedgefield covered his face with his hands and bowed his head.

There were guns on Chelsea 426, safely locked away in the colony's armoury. They were a remnant from the days when the colony was attached to the IMC's mining facility, when piracy was still a concern. They had never been used, and had not left the armoury in perhaps twenty years or more.

'Unlock the armoury,' he said, after an age. 'Tell Sergeant Bashford and his men to unlock the armoury and defend the colony at once!'

Was it possible that the soldiers who had unnervingly appeared out of thin air were pirates? If so, why had they come here? What did Chelsea 426 have that they might steal?

Mayor Sedgefield stood up and walked around his office in circles, rubbing his eyes with the palms of his hands.

'Mr Mayor.' Another voice, this time female, and from another part of the colony.

'Yes,' he replied wearily.

'Mr Mayor, we are getting reports of a major incident at the Oxygen Gardens, sir.'

Sedgefield sighed, dropping himself back down into his chair. 'There is a major incident happening *everywhere*,' he said.

On the screens he saw all five officers of Chelsea 426's police force approaching the armoury. At their head, Sergeant Bashford opened the thick metal doors, and began passing out pulse rifles to his men.

'Sergeant Bashford,' said the Mayor.

On screen the Sergeant turned and looked directly up at the camera.

'Yes, Mr Mayor?'

'When you engage with our… *visitors*… please ask them what their demands are. Do not open fire on them unless…'

'Unless what, sir?'

'I… What I mean to say… Uh… Don't… I mean…'

What could he say? Nothing in all his years on the colony council had prepared him for this moment.

'Just ask them what they want,' he said eventually.

Sergeant Bashford nodded and then, closing the armoury doors, ordered his men to about-turn and make their way toward Miramont Gardens.

***

You have to hand it to them, the Doctor thought as he passed through the stampeding crowds of residents and visitors, *nobody knows how to panic quite like humans.*

He didn't want to compare them to sheep, as such – that would be vaguely insulting to both species, albeit for different reasons – but they certainly knew how to lose all reason and self-control in an emergency. Most of them, anyway.

He had left the Grand Hotel to find the colony far removed from the sedate and, yes, if he had to find a word, *boring* place that had first greeted him. What few conversations he could overhear amongst the noise of screaming and shouting were barely intelligible. Nobody seemed to have the first idea what was going on, and why should they? Of all those on board Chelsea 426 it was only the Doctor who grasped the seriousness of the situation.

'Smalls was right,' cried one old man as he ran past the Doctor, holding his trilby hat to his head. 'It's all these Newcomers, if you ask me!'

The moment the Sontaran ship had first come into view, the pieces of the puzzle had begun to mesh in the Doctor's mind. The chemical composition of the spores, the behaviour of Mrs Carstairs, Mr Pemberton and the others. He knew full well what it all meant. All the Doctor could hope was that he got to the Sontarans before any of the residents did.

That hope was dashed the moment he left Tunbridge

Street and ran out into Miramont Gardens. On one side of the square, standing shoulder to shoulder in rows of ten, were the Sontarans. On the other side stood five policemen armed with rifles.

One of the policemen, their leader the Doctor imagined, stepped forward.

'I am Sergeant Bashford of the Chelsea 426 constabulary,' he said. 'We mean you no harm. Please state your intent.'

For a moment the Sontarans stood immobile and silent. They appeared almost like statues, like some latter-day Terracotta Army. Finally one of their fold left the group and marched towards the Sergeant, his feet stomping heavily on the metal floor.

'Sergeant Bashford,' a voice barked from inside the helmet, 'I am Colonel Sarg of the Fourth Sontaran Intelligence Division. We have orders to search this facility for all known enemies of Sontar. Do you allow us to proceed?'

'Um,' said Sergeant Bashford, looking back at his men, helplessly. He turned back to face the Sontaran, 'Colonel... Colonel...?'

'Sarg,' said the Sontaran.

'Colonel Sarg... We are a peaceful colony and mean you no harm.'

'Whether you mean us harm or not is of little consequence,' said Sarg, and then, more forcefully, 'Do you allow us to proceed?'

The Doctor was now at the edge of the gardens, trying his best to go unnoticed as he made his way stealthily towards the policemen.

'You have no enemies here,' said Sergeant Bashford. 'This colony is the property of the Powe-Luna Corporation. Its inhabitants are human. We mean you no—'

'Silence!' barked Colonel Sarg. 'Your babbling indicates an unwillingness to comply. You are armed, Sergeant Bashford, are you not?'

'I… er…' Bashford stuttered, looking down at his rifle.

'You are armed, sir!' yelled Colonel Sarg.

The Doctor looked from the handful of police officers to the Sontarans. He knew all too well what was about to happen.

'No!' he shouted, breaking his cover and running towards Sergeant Bashford. 'Drop your weapons! Drop them now!'

Sergeant Bashford turned to face the Doctor, his shaking hands still grasping his rifle, and still the Doctor ran, holding up his hands in one last, desperate gesture.

Sarg turned to the front row of his command.

'Sontarans,' he growled. 'Open fire!'

The front row of the unit lifted their weapons in one swift move, and suddenly the square was lit up crimson with the flare of a dozen laser beams. The bolts of blood-red light cut across the square in a sweeping arc. Sergeant Bashford and his men were massacred in an instant.

'No!' the Doctor shouted, falling to his knees where their bodies now lay. As the smoke and the smell of burnt flesh cleared, he looked up from the dead and saw the Sontarans marching toward him, their guns still ready to fire.

EIGHT

With his chin resting on his desk and his lower lip jutting out in a helpless pout, Mayor Sedgefield lifted the ball at one end of his Newton's Cradle desk toy, and let go. It swung down, hit the next ball along, which in turn kicked the ball at the end of a row of five up into the air, before it swung back down, starting the process all over again.

Click-clack-click-clack-click-clack…

'Mr Mayor…'

He couldn't even bear to look at the screens any more. He dreaded to think what might be happening outside his offices. He was only glad those offices were soundproof.

'Mr Mayor…'

He looked up at the door and saw one of his assistants. She looked scared, terrified even, her eyes bloodshot from crying and her cheeks streaked with mascara.

'Yes?' said Mayor Sedgefield.

'Mr Mayor... *sir*... The leader of the... Well, I'm not sure what they are, sir... But he's here, sir... To see you.'

Mayor Sedgefield sat upright, his mouth open, his eyes wide with fear. After looking around the room for an alternative exit that he knew did not exist, he nodded.

'Show him in.'

Seconds later they came through the door – three of the soldiers in blue armour, one marching in front with a long baton tucked under his arm, and two following closely behind. The leader stopped when he reached the Mayor's desk.

'Are *you* the administrator of this facility?' he bellowed.

Sedgefield answered him with a trembling lower lip but no words.

'Sir,' said the soldier. 'Are you the leader of this colony?'

Sedgefield nodded, bracing himself with both hands on his desk to stop himself from shaking.

The soldier lifted up its gloved hands, which the Mayor noticed had only three digits, and, with a mechanical hiss, lifted off his helmet to reveal a hideous, egg-shaped bald head. Placing his helmet down on the desk with a heavy thud, the alien soldier reached forward. Mayor Sedgefield released his vice-like grip from the desk and nervously shook the creature's hand.

'I am General Kade, Commander of the Fourth Sontaran Intelligence Division,' said the creature.

'I… I… I'm Mayor Sedgefield,' said the Mayor. 'Um… pleased to meet you?'

'Mayor Sedgefield,' Kade continued, 'our intelligence leads us to understand that your colony has been taken over by an enemy of ours.'

'R-really?' Sedgefield stuttered.

'Yes,' replied the Sontaran. 'We have been at war with a race known as the Rutan Host for nearly fifty thousand of your years. They are master spies, sir, and a menace. It is our intention to search this colony and eliminate every single Rutan on board.'

The Mayor fell back into his chair, his head in his hands.

'Mayor Sedgefield,' said Kade. 'What few defences you had have been neutralised. Your limited weapons are in our possession. Your exits are sealed. We have surrounded the colony with a propagation mirror so that no communications may leave this facility. All docking systems have been locked so that no spacecraft may escape. You have no choice in this matter.'

'B-b-b-but there aren't any aliens here,' said the Mayor. 'Only humans. We… we're the only ones here.'

'The Rutans are, as I have said, master spies. They will appear quite human, but we are of the understanding that there may already be several thousand of them. We intend to find them and destroy them, Mayor Sedgefield, and then we shall leave you in...' Kade sneered, as if the word he was about to say were somehow poisonous to him, '*peace.*'

Sedgefield looked up through the domed glass ceiling of his office. The Sontaran ship was now hovering, in orbit, only a few hundred metres away. He had little doubt that they could destroy the whole of Chelsea 426 in the blink of an eye if they wanted to.

'Do I... do I have your word?' he asked, finally looking Kade in the eye.

'Of course, sir,' said Kade. 'A Sontaran's word is his bond.'

'Not strictly true that, is it?' said a voice from the other side of the office.

Kade and the Mayor turned to see Colonel Sarg entering the room with a prisoner.

'Who is this?' Kade snapped.

'We arrested him nearby, sir,' said Sarg, nudging his prisoner forward by digging the barrel of his rifle into the man's back. 'He demanded he be allowed to speak to you.'

Kade snorted dismissively.

'Oh, did he now?' He turned to the prisoner. 'And who *are* you exactly?'

'Oh, I'm the Doctor. And you are?'

'I am General Kade, of the Fourth Sontaran Intelligence Division.'

'The Fourth Sontaran *Intelligence Division*?' asked the Doctor.

'Yes,' grunted Kade. 'You have heard of us?'

'No,' said the Doctor. 'No, not at all. Just seems like a bit of an oxymoron, if you ask me.'

'Well I didn't,' snapped Kade. 'Did you say that you are the Doctor?'

'Yep,' replied the Doctor. 'That's me.'

It was then that the Sontaran did something the Doctor clearly hadn't expected.

He smiled.

'Well,' said Kade, still beaming. 'That really is quite something, is it not?'

'Oh,' said the Doctor, shifting awkwardly. 'Is it?'

'We have travelled so far for this mission, and here you are… the Doctor.'

Kade now began pacing around the room, looking up at the Doctor as if he were a specimen in a museum.

'Fascinating,' he said. 'Absolutely fascinating.' He turned to Sarg. 'Colonel Sarg… Do you know who this is?'

'No, sir,' replied Sarg. 'I hadn't seen him before his arrest, sir.'

'This,' said Kade, 'is the Doctor. A face-changer who travels through time. Our race have encountered him many times, usually within this system, and he has, without fail, bested us. So far. Quite remarkable. Quite, quite remarkable.'

'Right,' said the Doctor. 'Well… Now that we've got the introductory chitchat over and done with, what are you doing here?'

Kade suddenly lashed out with his baton, hitting the Doctor in the arm.

'Ow!' the Doctor yelled.

'Please understand,' said Kade, 'that my respect for you as an adversary does not allow you to address me as you would a subordinate or a small child.'

'Understood,' said the Doctor, still holding his arm and wincing.

'We are here,' Kade continued, 'because our enemy, the Rutan Host, is using this facility as a staging post for a counter-attack upon Sontar.'

'The Rutans!' said the Doctor, his face lighting up. 'I knew it! I knew it was the Rutans. It was the carbon levels. *Far* too high for a Krynoid. And then the speech thing, with the words… "That will be agreeable." Pure Rutan slip-up, that one. Pure, good old-fash—'

'Be quiet!' shouted Kade, lifting up the baton but holding back from hitting the Doctor a second time. 'As I was saying… The Rutans are using this facility as a staging post for a counter-attack upon Sontar…'

'Permission to speak?' said the Doctor, holding up his hand.

'Permission granted.'

'A counter-attack? What have you done to them lately? I mean… Apart from a war spanning fifty millennia and all the rest of it.'

'Our attempt,' said Kade, 'to utilise the Earth as a breeding centre for further armies. When the Rutans discovered that Earth was to become a cloning facility for the Sontaran Empire they planted a trap on a neighbouring world – this world. A sentient spore that, when brought into a habitable environment, would grow into plants, producing further spores. These spores, Doctor, are the Rutans themselves.'

'OK,' said the Doctor. 'I *think* I'm with you so far, but can't the Rutans shape-shift? Why go to all this bother to get breathed in by humans, or Sontarans, or whoever, when they could have just *turned themselves* into humans or Sontarans?'

'We are not as primitive as you think, Doctor. Their technology was crude and often fallible. We have the technology to tell Sontaran from Rutan, regardless of shape and size. The Rutans are a breed of parasites, Doctor… For them it was far more fitting to exploit a host. In their plan those hosts would have been Sontarans from the nearby clone world that was once Earth. In the event, the birthing planet was not to happen, and the humans got here first.'

The Doctor allowed himself a moment's thought.

'OK, OK…' he said, 'but that means you're unable to

scan for anyone who might have breathed in the Rutan spore, doesn't it?'

'Quite right, Doctor.'

'So then,' said the Doctor, 'how are you going to… well, you know… root out the Rutans? Ha… I quite like that. Root out the Rutans. Sounds like a board game, or something, doesn't it?'

Colonel Sarg now stepped forward and, in a hushed voice, said, 'General… What he says is true. Would it not be wise, if we are unable to tell the difference between human and Rutan, to simply destroy the whole colony? It would eliminate any possibility of the Rutans escaping, sir.'

'Oh no,' said the Doctor. 'I heard that. No. No no no no no. You can't do that. I *know* there are Rutans here. I saw what they did, and we need to sort this out, but no… No. I won't let you kill people.'

Kade turned to the Doctor and raised one hairless eyebrow quizzically.

'Won't *let* me?' he said. 'As I see it, Doctor, you have no say in the matter. Soldiers… Take him away.'

'Wait!' said the Doctor, as two of the Sontarans held him by the arms and dragged him toward the door. 'Where are they taking me?'

'Wherever you wish to go,' said General Kade. 'Our quarrel is not with you. You have been our adversary in the past and, as I have said, you have bested us. On this occasion that is not an option available to you. I would strongly recommend you leave this colony as quickly as you arrived. You are, after all, the only one who can.'

'You can't kill them!' said the Doctor. 'They're unarmed. Where is the honour in that, General? Didn't you say you were the Intelligence Division?'

Kade gestured at the guards to stop dragging him away.

'I did, sir.'

'Well… Not very intelligent, just blowing this place up, is it?' said the Doctor. 'I mean… You *are* meant to be *intelligence*, after all. Surely it would be much more *intelligent* to find out who the Rutans are first before you make any rash decisions?'

Kade looked from the Doctor to Colonel Sarg and then back to the Doctor.

"You may be right,' he said, and then, turning back to Sarg, 'Order all Rutan suspects to be placed into custody immediately.'

Sensing a moment's pause, Mayor Sedgefield held up his hand like a schoolboy and leaned into Kade's field of view.

'Er, hello… Yes… Er, we have visitors,' he said, 'Newcomers. They were guests for the Flower Show. From what you were saying… It sounds as if the Flower Show is where these friends of yours… the, er, Rutans, wasn't it?'

'The Rutans are no friends of Sontar!' barked General Kade.

HURON PUBLIC LIBRARY
521 DAKOTA AVE S
HURON, SD 57350

'No… Well, er, quite… But what I was going to say was… If anyone here on Chelsea 426 *is* a Rutan, it will be them. The Newcomers, I mean. The people on the ships. The ones who were at the Flower Show.'

'Splendid!' said Kade, slamming one hand on the desk. 'You have been most cooperative! Guards, take the Doctor away. We have no further need of him.'

The entrance to the office opened with a mechanical hum, and the Sontarans clutched the Doctor by the arms once again, pulling him away from the Mayor and General Kade. He could have fought against them, but there was no point. He had to get back to the Grand Hotel, and quickly.

NINE

'You gave me quite a fright there,' said Mr Carstairs, gently placing one hand on his wife's shoulder.

She had been gazing out of the window of the hotel bar at the Western Docks for an age, silent and expressionless. The Doctor's words echoed in Mr Carstairs' mind, about her not being his wife. He didn't believe a word of it. What did this Doctor know, anyway? Whatever had happened at the Flower Show, the Doctor's explanation seemed so far-fetched, so ridiculous. There had to be a rational explanation, and one that did not involve his wife being a creature from another planet. He had a good mind to turf the Doctor out the moment he returned. The colony had been a perfectly peaceful place until his arrival.

'Bess?' said Mr Carstairs, taking his hand away.

Mrs Carstairs turned to face him and smiled.

'Yes, dear?'

'I said you gave me quite a fright, there.'

'Did I, dear?'

'Yes. Yes, you did. You were out cold.'

She smiled again.

'Well I'm feeling much better now,' she said. 'Just a little tired, that's all.'

'I see,' said Mr Carstairs. 'Well just so long as you're OK.'

'And where are the children?'

'They're out in the lobby with the Major. He's holding the fort. He reckoned he was going to get his gun and show those… those people a thing or two, but I talked him out of it.'

'Good,' said Mrs Carstairs. 'Good.'

Mr Carstairs heard footsteps from the other side of the room and turned to see the Doctor.

'You…' hissed Mr Carstairs. 'I'm only surprised you've got the nerve to show your face here. After those *things* turned up. Who *are* they, anyway?'

The Doctor walked across the bar slowly and sat next to Mr Carstairs.

'They're Sontarans,' he said. 'A clone race from the planet Sontar. Bred for war. A whole race of soldiers.'

'Nonsense!'

'It's not. Trust me, it's not.' The Doctor turned to

Mrs Carstairs. 'You know what I'm talking about, don't you?'

Mrs Carstairs frowned and then smiled politely.

'I'm afraid I don't have the slightest idea what you mean, Doctor,' she said.

'Of course you don't,' said the Doctor, and then, more coldly, 'The people on this colony are going to die unless you meet the Sontarans head-on.'

She frowned again and laughed dismissively.

'I'm sorry, Doctor, but what do you mean?'

'Stop using them,' the Doctor snapped. 'This isn't their war. They didn't ask to be used like this. The Sontarans are out there, right now, rounding up the visitors from their ships and holding them captive. Goodness knows what they'll do to them.'

'Newcomers?' said Mr Carstairs. 'They're rounding up the Newcomers?'

The Doctor nodded.

'Well it's a good thing they are,' Mr Carstairs continued. 'If you ask me it's the Newcomers who've *caused* all this fuss and bother. We had no trouble here until they turned up. Or until *you* turned up, for that matter, Doctor.'

'It's *not* the Newcomers,' said the Doctor, gritting his teeth. 'It's an alien species. They're called the Rutan Host. They've been at war with the Sontarans for tens of thousands of years, and they're using the spores, the ones found by Professor Wilberforce, to take over the people here. Visitors and residents alike.'

Mr Carstairs laughed, shaking his head. 'And you expect us to believe that? You're accusing my wife of being one of these... these... what did you call them?'

'Rutans,' said the Doctor.

'Do you hear that, Bess?' said Mr Carstairs. 'You're a Rutan. Have you ever heard anything so preposterous in your life?'

Mrs Carstairs said nothing.

'If they round up the Newcomers and take them away, we'll just be rid of a lot of unwanted company,' Mr Carstairs went on, 'and there'll hardly be a person on the colony who disagrees with me.'

Just then Jake and Vienna ran into the bar. They stopped a short distance from their parents and the Doctor, as if sensing the icy tension between the three adults.

'Mum, Dad,' said Jake. 'Come out here... There's something on TV. About what's happening.'

The Doctor was the first to stand, running out into the lobby with the children. They were joined eventually by Mr and Mrs Carstairs.

From the video screen above the seating area in the lobby, the face of Riley Smalls sneered down on them.

'So,' said the presenter, one eyebrow raised in a laconic arch, 'I hate to say "I told you so", but...'

He paused, sitting back in his large leather chair with folded arms.

'Our visitors say that we have been invaded,' Smalls continued. 'And have I not said this all along? Right now the Sontaran army, for that is their name, are out there rounding up the Newcomers. Are any of us surprised? Here on Chelsea 426 we have enjoyed years of peace and prosperity, and the moment any Newcomers turn up, en masse, we have *this*! Scenes of chaos and disruption on the streets of our tranquil home. Residents running for their lives.

'It seems quite clear to me now that the Sontarans are not our enemies. The Sontarans are our allies in this, our darkest hour. Unlike the Newcomers who, it transpires, are vicious and conniving *aliens*... Yes, you heard me correctly... *aliens*... The Sontarans are a proud and noble race who mean us *no harm*.

'I say we should help them and assist them in their work. If you, or anyone you know, have Newcomers staying with you, you must report them immediately. They may have come with smiles and good manners, but that does not mean they are to be trusted. The good citizens of Chelsea 426 have nothing to hide and therefore nothing to fear from the Sontarans. Only if we allow them to investigate this matter properly will we ever enjoy the happy and contented lives to which we were formerly accustomed.'

The Doctor clapped his hand to his forehead and groaned.

'Do you see?' said Mr Carstairs. 'I was right. They're

saying so on the television now, Doctor. It's the *Newcomers* who have brought this on us.'

'You're going to listen to *him*?' said the Doctor. 'Riley Smallbrain? Oh, please… The man has the IQ of an amoeba.'

'He happens to be a very intelligent man,' said Mr Carstairs. 'But I can't say I'm surprised that you doubt him. After all, you happen to be a Newcomer yourself.'

'Intelligent?' said the Doctor. 'Him? But he's a *Cryogen.*'

'Oh, I see,' said Mr Carstairs. 'Full of empathy and understanding, except when it comes to Cryogens. Well… I certainly didn't realise we had a Cryophobe staying with us…'

'It's not… Wait. *Cryophobe?* Is that even a real word? No, Mr Carstairs… I'm quite serious. Riley Smalls is an early twenty-first-century Cryogen. The process they used in those days was flawed. The people they brought out of cryogenic suspension suffered massive, irreversible brain damage. Which perhaps makes my Smallbrain joke a bit tasteless, but that doesn't alter the fact… You can't take his word for it. Cryogens are renowned for having poor judgement. They're hasty, bad-tempered and most of all they're very, very confused. The poor man must have come here before the people on Earth realised. Most of the Cryogens there live in nursing homes.'

'Well,' said Mr Carstairs, 'Whatever you may think

of Mr Smalls and his views, the fact remains, we have nothing to hide so we have nothing to fear. Those Sontarans aren't coming for us, are they?'

'No,' said the Doctor gravely. 'Not yet.'

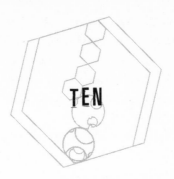

TEN

'If you could all please remain calm,' said Captain Thomas, walking among the passengers on the deck, his voice as calm and reassuring as it could be, given the circumstances. 'I'm sure there is nothing for us to worry about.'

It was Zack and Jenny's honeymoon. They had saved up for almost a year to pay for their tickets and even then, even when they had received an 'extra bit of help' from their parents, they had only been able to afford a cabin in the lower decks of the *Pride of Deimos*. Still, that had been enough for Jenny.

Their journey to the sky dock near 588 Achilles seemed a very distant memory now. They had held hands practically the whole way and, as they'd landed and the great silver cruise ship came into view, Jenny had thought she might burst with joy. Zack had done a good job of keeping his emotions to himself, as he always did, but she was sure she saw the slightest flicker of a boyish grin and the budding of tears in his eyes when they first saw it.

The *Pride of Deimos* was, in every sense, a billion miles away from home. Zack worked on the T-Rails, programming destinations from the central hub, and Jenny worked in an AlphaMart on the outskirts of the city. People like them didn't normally get to set foot on a ship like the *Pride of Deimos*, let alone sail on her.

As they passed through the air-locked bridge and into the ship, all Jenny could say was, 'I can't believe it. I just can't believe it.'

The ship itself was like a fairy tale: twinkling chandeliers and ornate fountains at every turn. The other passengers spoke in clipped colony accents, the kind Jenny had only ever heard in films or on television. They were nothing like the people back home. Zack, meanwhile, acted as if he were only mildly impressed, though Jenny could tell that deep down he was as excited and as awestruck as she was.

From the Trojan Asteroids the ship had taken them out past Jupiter, where they flew over the tumultuous carmine vortex of the Great Red Spot at a distance of just a few hundred thousand kilometres. They had passed the Galilean Moons, watched volcanoes erupt on Io, and had gazed down upon the scarred ice fields of Europa as they glistened in the sunlight like a endless ocean of crystal.

Even the intervals of empty space, black and seemingly limitless, that lay between the asteroids, planets and moons had a strange beauty about them. It was humbling to think of their home back on Earth, floating in this vast and infinite wasteland.

When the Captain had announced they were making an unscheduled stop on Saturn, the passengers were elated. There had been talk back on Earth of the plants discovered there, a rare thing these days. It wasn't often that news from the colonies made much of a splash back home, but this had stirred the imaginations of many. Jenny had never thought she and Zack might be among the privileged few to actually *be there* to find out what all the fuss was about. Now their excitement and their joy seemed like little more than the set-up to a cruel joke with a savage punchline.

The passengers were gathered on the deck of the *Pride of Deimos*, beneath the almost invisible protection of the force fields, but hardly anybody spoke, and when they did it was with hushed concern.

'What do you think's happening?' Jenny asked, gripping Zack's hand as tightly as she could.

Zack shrugged.

'Your guess is as good as mine,' he said. 'Maybe it's a fire alarm or something.'

'A fire?' said Jenny.

Zack squeezed her hand and smiled.

'Not a *fire*,' he said. 'Just an alarm. I'm sure there's nothing to worry about, just like the Captain said.'

His words were sadly contradicted by the appearance of the soldiers, although they were unlike any soldiers Jenny or Zack had ever seen before.

They came up onto the deck, marching in file: squat men in metallic blue armour, their faces hidden beneath domed helmets.

The passengers collectively gasped, and Captain Thomas immediately ran across the deck toward the new arrivals.

'What's happening?' he asked. 'What *is* this?'

One of the soldiers stepped forward and addressed Thomas directly.

'I am Colonel Sarg of the Fourth Sontaran Intelligence Division. Are you the Captain of this vessel?'

The Captain nodded.

'Then I hereby commandeer this ship in the name of Sontar. Your passengers must disembark immediately, under our custody, and will remain our prisoners until our investigation is complete.'

'Investigation?' said Thomas. 'Now you look here…'

'Captain, that is not a request; it is an order.'

The Sontaran lifted his rifle and aimed it squarely at the Captain's head. Hearing the weapon power up with a faint hum that rose in pitch, Captain Thomas looked to his crew, and then back at the armoured creature before him. With great reluctance he closed his eyes and nodded.

The Sontarans marched out onto the deck and formed a circle around the passengers.

'Oh no,' said Jenny. 'What's going to happen to us?'

'It's going to be OK,' said Zack. 'Everything's going to be OK.'

It had always been a possibility.

Indeed, their original plans had counted on the Sontarans arriving on Saturn to mine for hydrogen, and so this was not so much a hindrance as a slight alteration to the itinerary.

Professor Wilberforce sat in his office, watching events unfold in the colony on the thin glass monitor in the centre of his desk. He laughed as he saw the Sontarans board each of the visiting ships, rounding up the passengers and leading them down into the loading bays and docking areas.

The Sontarans were such a mindless, brutish race. They lacked the finesse and the sophistication of the collective Rutan mind. They were clones but, in his opinion, clones bred from inferior stock. The Rutans were their superiors in every way imaginable, only ever submitting to their age-old enemy when it was tactically appropriate, or when they were met with the sheer force of numbers that the Sontarans could muster.

It was this latest plan which allowed the Rutans to match that force of numbers, even if their hosts were human. If they could now reach the Earth, an Earth which had not been conquered by the Sontarans, there would be ten billion potential hosts for them to exploit, with all the spacecraft and weaponry that the humans had at their disposal.

Five hundred years earlier, the humans had been no match for the Sontarans and yet, from what little information Wilberforce had managed to access, it would appear they had somehow defeated them. Imagine what might be possible now, now that their evolution had progressed so much.

The Sontarans wouldn't stand a chance.

'Professor Wilberforce…'

His idle daydreaming was interrupted by the voice of Alice, standing in the doorway, her expression cool and impassive.

'Yes, Alice?'

'They are here.'

'I thought as much. Our thoughts become stronger, do they not?'

'Yes, Professor. Their leader, a General Kade, is demanding he speak to us. By which we mean he wishes to speak with Professor Wilberforce.'

'Well, it was to be expected. Do they suspect anything?'

Alice laughed.

'No, Professor. That fool of a Mayor has told them to search the visitors' ships.'

Now it was Professor Wilberforce's turn to laugh.

'Yes,' he said. 'We saw them on the monitor. Quite amusing, really. Well, you should probably show him in.'

Alice smiled, nodded, and left the office. Moments later she returned with the Sontaran leader.

He entered the office with the typical Sontaran air of self-importance, his baton tucked under his arm, and stood before the Professor.

'Professor Wilberforce?' he growled.

'Yes,' said Wilberforce, getting to his feet and extending his hand. The Sontaran shook it forcefully.

'I am General Kade, of the Fourth Sontaran Intelligence Division. We have begun rounding up the visitors from their ships. We have reason to believe that the plants you have grown may be instrumental in a plot against our race.'

The Professor feigned surprise.

'Is that so?' he asked. 'Well, that's… that's astounding.'

Kade's attention had now turned to the plant in the corner of the office.

'Is that one of them?' he asked, pointing toward the glass dome with his baton.

The Professor nodded.

Kade walked around the desk and made his way to

the far corner, crouching on his haunches next to the glass dome containing the plant.

'Fascinating,' he said. 'Such an innocuous-looking thing, isn't it?'

'Well, quite,' said Wilberforce.

'We will of course be seizing this as a part of our investigation,' Kade continued.

'But of course.'

Kade turned to the Professor, his lips curling into what might have been a smile.

'You are most helpful,' he said. 'And wise. I must say, we had expected greater resistance from the inhabitants of this outpost, but we have been pleasantly surprised by your compliance.'

Professor Wilberforce smiled in return.

'Anything we can do to help,' he said.

Neither Zack nor Jenny had spoken since they had left the *Pride of Deimos* and been taken down into the dimly lit confines of the loading bay. Zack had not let go of Jenny's hand, and she had noticed his grip tighten each time one of the Sontarans barked at them to 'move along'. The other passengers were chattering nervously and Jenny heard one, an elegant older woman in pearls, repeatedly asking what was going to happen to her luggage. It had only then occurred to Jenny that *their* luggage was still on the ship, but it was a thought that passed quickly. Who cared what was going to happen to their luggage? There were far more important things for them to worry about right now.

When all of the passengers had left the ship and were gathered in the loading bay, the large doors behind them slammed shut with an echoing clang and the room fell silent. In a corner of the bay a door opened, spilling light out into the gloom, and more of the Sontarans marched in, accompanied by humans.

One of the humans was a tall, older man, wearing half-moon spectacles and dressed in a white lab coat. At his side was a younger woman, slightly built with her mousy brown hair tied back.

'This way, Professor,' said one of the Sontarans to the older man. 'You have your instruments?'

The Professor nodded.

'Yes,' he said. 'But I really don't see why I'm needed here. I am a botanist, General Kade, not a physician.'

The Sontaran leader stopped abruptly and looked up at the Professor.

'You say that machine of yours can be used to detect any trace of the spores?'

The Professor nodded, holding up a small, black spherical device, no larger than an apple, out of which there emerged a short rubber hose capped by a nozzle.

'Yes,' said the Professor, quizzically.

'Then you must test each of these visitors,' said General Kade. 'If they have inhaled the spore, there will still be traces, will there not?'

The Professor nodded.

'Then test them, man. Test them!' barked Kade.

Dutifully, the Professor approached the crowd of passengers and, walking past them one by one, he held up the nozzle of the device and began taking samples from the air around them, occasionally looking back at the Sontaran leader.

Kade turned to the Professor's assistant.

'You, girl,' he said.

'My name's Alice,' the young woman replied.

'That is of no importance to me!' said Kade. 'Are there more of these instruments?' He gestured toward the Professor with his baton.

'Yes, back at the gardens,' said Alice.

'Then bring them to me,' said Kade. 'We shall be here for eons, otherwise. Time is of the essence.'

'Of course,' said Alice, smiling politely. 'That would be agreeable.'

She had turned and was halfway towards the loading bay exit when Kade turned back.

'What did you say?' he asked.

Alice stopped in her tracks, and turned very slowly so that she now faced Kade once more.

'I'm sorry…?'

'What did you just say?'

Alice smiled nervously.

'Nothing… I just said, "Of course".'

'After that. What did you say?'

Alice looked beyond the Sontaran now, at the Professor, who had turned away from the passengers and was slowly drawing a glass thermometer from the pocket of his lab coat.

They held each other's gaze for a moment and then, in one sudden, violent move, the Professor thrust the thermometer into the neck of one of the Sontaran soldiers.

Peering over the shoulders of those standing around her, Jenny saw the thermometer jutting out from a narrow hole in the back of the soldier's armour. The soldier staggered forward, clutching at the back of its neck with both hands, and making a terrible gurgling sound in its throat.

The Professor lunged forward again and tugged at the thermometer, snapping it in half. The Sontaran howled in pain as globules of mercury fell from the broken glass, before collapsing to the ground, its last breath leaving it with a sickening rattle.

Now the young woman, Alice, ran towards General Kade, a scalpel in her hand, howling monstrously, as if she were possessed. The General reached out with his baton, which emitted a sudden flashing bolt of orange energy, and Alice fell to the ground, doubled over in pain.

The Sontarans now had both her and the Professor separately surrounded.

The Professor looked down at Alice, and then across

the loading bay at General Kade, breathing heavily, but with a malevolent smile. Cackling maniacally, Wilberforce held up his hands, white sparks of electricity jumping from his fingertips but, before he could make his move, the Sontarans opened fire, the red flare of a dozen laser beams cutting him down until he lay in a smoking heap at their feet.

Alice let out a mournful wail, reaching up towards Kade pathetically, the blade of the scalpel pointing up at him, before a second ear-splitting barrage of lasers silenced her.

It was a silence that would last just seconds before the passengers and the crew of the *Pride of Deimos* began to scream.

Sneering callously, General Kade made his way toward the loading bay exit.

He turned to one of his subordinates and snarled, 'Interrogate them using all means necessary, and then inform Colonel Sarg that *all* humans on the colony are to be arrested immediately. It's worse than we thought.' Kade marched out of the loading bay, the double doors closing behind him with a thunderous clang.

The remaining Sontarans turned on their heels and, lifting up their weapons, began marching toward the unarmed passengers.

Zack turned to Jenny and put his arms around her, holding her close.

'I love you,' he said.

'I love you too,' said Jenny.

He smiled down at her and gently wiped a tear from her cheek as the Sontarans drew closer and closer.

ELEVEN

Gazing into his dressing-room mirror, Riley Smalls straightened his tie and ran one hand through his thinning hair. Somewhere outside the studio he could hear the howls of the sirens, rendered faint and barely audible by the thick walls.

This, he had decided, was his moment. Back on Earth, before his cryogenic suspension and a long time before he awoke in a different century, he had dreamed of the day when he would report an event of great importance. His television show had given him the opportunity to discuss news events, politics and wars, but never anything like this.

For the first time in a very long while, Riley Smalls was excited. He liked life on the colony, there was no doubt about that, but it was hardly exciting. He had made the decision to abandon Earth and move there for good only a few months after coming out of cryogenic suspension. The planet that had greeted him on his waking had been quite different to the one he had left behind. It was so crowded and the people there so different. The everyday things that he had taken for granted no longer existed. The things that he thought of as timeless traditions were now little more than footnotes in history.

The counsellors provided by the cryogenics lab had tried to tell him that this was simply the way of the world – that times changed and that things came to pass – but he was having none of it. As far as he was concerned, the world had forcibly been changed by the very people he had railed against in his television show. They, it would seem, had won, and left the world an overcrowded and chaotic mess. When the opportunity arose to pack his bags and leave for Saturn, he had seized it in an instant.

But then a strange thing happened. Days smudged into weeks and months and eventually years, and he came to realise that he was bored. For years now his show, *The Smalls Agenda*, had largely involved him pouring scorn upon a planet more than a billion miles away, based upon the titbits of information they received on the weekly news broadcasts. He began to see his role as little more than a comforting reminder to the inhabitants of Chelsea 426 that they had made the right choice, leaving Earth, and that it was so terrible there they would never want to go back.

All that had changed with the discovery of the spores and the arrival of the Newcomers. Now there were people on Chelsea 426 for him to rail against. Now his words would make a difference.

Truth was, the Newcomers terrified him. Chelsea 426, as boring as it might have been, was a comfortable oasis of calm. Its environment was so carefully constructed to remind the inhabitants of a time and a place that was, so they imagined, less troubling and changeable, that the arrival of any reminder that the rest of the universe was not that way troubled him. It hung over him like a dark storm cloud, overshadowing his thoughts and emotions.

However sudden and uninvited the appearance of these Sontarans was, they spoke of ridding the colony of invaders, and that was good enough for him.

'Mr Smalls, they're ready for you.'

It was one of his show's runners standing in the doorway of his dressing room. He faced her with a disarming smile and nodded, rising from his chair and following her out into the corridor.

In the studio he sat behind a wide grey desk, before a blue and red backdrop. One of the sound technicians clipped a tiny microphone to the lapel of his jacket, and the make-up artist gave him a last-minute dab of powder on the nose. Behind the camera, the director counted down, 'Five, four,' and then mimed the rest of the countdown with his fingers.

Three. Two. One.

'Greetings,' said Smalls, smiling into the camera. 'As some of you may be aware, our honourable guests, the Sontarans, are investigating a serious incident here on our colony. At first they arrested our so-called visitors, the Newcomers, from their ships and hotels. Now, it transpires, they are arresting the residents of Chelsea 426.

'Now there are some out there who will say that they are overstepping the mark, that they are trampling over our liberties, but to this I say: Nonsense! The Sontarans are a proud and noble people who just so happen to be at war with a venomous and parasitic race called the Rutans. Right now we happen to be caught up in that war. Granted, it is through no fault of our own, but that isn't to say that we can simply stick our heads in the sand and pretend it isn't happening. The good citizens of Chelsea 426 have nothing to worry about. It is the Newcomers who have brought the war to us; not our people, and certainly not the Sontarans, and so it is the Newcomers who will suffer. Arrest and questioning by the Sontarans is but a minor inconvenience if we are to have stability return to our once happy colony.

'What you must ask yourselves is, do you want stability? Do you want peace? Are you so arrogant that you believe these things will simply be handed to you on a plate, or do you believe, as I do, that sacrifices must be made?

'Could you hold your head high with any sense of pride if you knew that, cometh the day, you had taken the coward's way out? That you had kowtowed to such a vile and poisonous species as the Rutans? Furthermore…'

He paused, taking in a deep breath. Then he was interrupted very suddenly by a crashing sound somewhere on the other side of the studio. Peering past the studio lights, shielding his eyes from the glare with his hand, he saw dark figures entering the room: dark, broad-shouldered figures brandishing guns. One by one, the technicians and assistants from his programme were being dragged out of the studio, marched at gunpoint through the exits. Finally one of the shadowy figures stepped into the light. It was a Sontaran.

'We have orders to take you into custody,' said the soldier.

'What?' said Smalls, getting to his feet and unclipping his microphone as quickly as he could.

'You are a Rutan suspect and as such will be taken into custody.'

'No,' said Smalls, backing away from the creature, waving his hands desperately as if this might ward off the Sontaran. 'No, there must be some mistake. I have supported your investigation from the beginning. What is this? You can't *arrest* me. I'm Riley Smalls, for crying out loud. Don't you know who I am? Where is your commanding officer? I demand to speak to your superi—'

His words were cut off suddenly and violently as a second Sontaran grabbed him from behind, covering his mouth with a gloved hand, and jabbing him in the back with the barrel of a gun.

Smalls felt his wrists locked together suddenly with handcuffs. Seconds later, he was blinded as one of the Sontarans tied a length of cloth around his face and over his eyes before wrapping another around his mouth, gagging him completely.

The cameras were still rolling, filming nothing but his empty chair, as they led him out of the studio.

TWELVE

'**B**ut why would they do that?' said Mr Carstairs, gazing up at the video screen in the lobby of the Grand Hotel. For a moment, there was little he could do but stand there, his mouth wide open, blinking up at the image of the desk and the empty chair in the seconds before it cut to static.

The Doctor appeared at his side.

'They were never going to stop with the Newcomers,' he said. 'It's not the Newcomers' fault. Like I said, this is their war – the Sontarans' and the Rutans' – not yours. But they've brought it here.'

'The Newcomers…' said Mr Carstairs, insistently.

The Doctor shook his head.

'But they *came* here…'

'They didn't make this happen. It was the plants, at the Flower Show. And the Sontarans will come here soon enough.'

'But... but... What can we do?'

It was a good question. What could they do? The Doctor could think of one very good way out. They could go to his room, get in the TARDIS, and leave – the Doctor, Mr and Mrs Carstairs, and their children, not forgetting the Major. But that would still leave every other visitor and resident on Chelsea 426 at the mercy of both the Sontarans and the Rutans. It wasn't an option.

'I could always get my gun,' said the Major, from his post behind the reception desk. 'A few blasts from my Maiman 4000 ought to show 'em a thing or two.'

Mr Carstairs turned to the Major and scowled.

'Oh, would you please shut up?' he snapped. 'I think we've all heard enough of your nonsense for one day, thank you very much. Your interminable war stories and your non-stop blathering on. You don't *have* a gun beneath your pillow, you old fool. You didn't have one when you checked in, and you don't have one now.'

The Major hung his head, his moustache twitching from side to side, but said nothing, choosing instead to pretend to read his newspaper.

Mr Carstairs sighed.

'The children,' he whispered to the Doctor. 'We need to... I mean... I don't want them to end up in the clutches of those... those *things*.'

'I won't let that happen,' said the Doctor.

'That thing,' Mr Carstairs continued. 'In your room. Your *ship*? Could that escape the colony?'

The Doctor nodded.

'Then I want you to get them out of here.'

'What?' said the Doctor. 'Just them? I could get you out of here, too, but… I don't know whether I can just leave while…'

Mr Carstairs closed his eyes and pinched the bridge of his nose between forefinger and thumb in deep concentration.

'I know… I know,' he said. 'I just… We can't leave the hotel. There's no saying what those things might do to the place. Somebody needs to stay here. I can't say I trust you wholeheartedly, Doctor. You're still a stranger to us. But I think I trust you enough, and I suppose that's the best we can hope for. Take the children as far away from here as you can. Somewhere *safe*.'

The Doctor nodded. He didn't want to leave Chelsea 426 any more than Mr Carstairs did, but the man was asking him to save his children, and placing all his trust in a person he neither knew nor particularly liked. That was enough for him.

'C'mon, kids,' said the Doctor, turning to the twins. 'We're going for a quick spin in a TARDIS. You too, Major.'

'Right-ho!' shouted the Major, walking out from behind the desk.

Jake followed the Major, and they walked toward the elevators. Vienna held back.

'You coming, Vienna?' said the Doctor, smiling in an effort to lift her spirits.

Vienna looked from the Doctor to her father, who was still watching the crackling white snow on the video screen, and then to her mother, who was gazing idly up through the lobby windows at the cruise ships anchored at the Western Docks.

'I… I don't know. Mum? Dad?'

Her mother didn't respond. Only her father turned to face her.

'Darling,' he said, 'please. Go with him. We'll be OK here. Trust me. I'm sure this will all be sorted out soon enough.'

He smiled as best he could, but Vienna saw the tears welling in his eyes.

Mr Carstairs turned to the Doctor and nodded; a subtle gesture but one loaded with much meaning. If he could have said anything more it would have been, 'Look after them.'

The elevator doors opened with a single chime, and the Doctor, the Major and the twins got in.

Seconds after they'd left, the Sontarans arrived, six of them in all. They marched into the lobby, their group leader approaching Mr Carstairs.

'In the name of Sontar, I place you under arrest. You are to come with us immediately.'

For the first time in an age, Mrs Carstairs turned away from the windows and looked directly at the Sontarans with the strangest flicker of a smile. Two of the Sontarans approached her, turning her violently before placing her wrists in metal cuffs.

'Bess!' shouted Mr Carstairs, turning to the group leader and punching him in the face. The creature's flesh was so much harder than he had imagined – more like a steel-toed leather boot than a human face – and the Sontaran barely flinched.

He struck Mr Carstairs with a baton and then stunned him with an electrifying bolt that he fired from one end of the weapon. Then he cuffed his prisoner and dragged him violently to his feet.

'This way,' the Sontaran grunted, marching Mr Carstairs toward the doors. Before they left the hotel the group leader turned to one of his team and said, 'Search the rest of the building. There may be others.'

'I say, old chap, where exactly are we going?' asked the Major as they stepped out of the elevator and into the corridor.

'To my room,' said the Doctor. 'My TARDIS... I mean, my ship is there. We're going to get these two out of here. You too, if you want to come along for the ride.'

'Mm,' the Major huffed. 'I'm not so sure about that. Beating a hasty retreat and whatnot. Sounds an awful lot like surrender, if you ask me. You know, this reminds me of the Siege of the Hexion Gates.'

'Really?' said the Doctor, failing to mask his lack of interest.

'Quite,' said the Major. 'A hundred of us stuck in the hull of an old B-Class Destroyer. The thing was riddled, looked like a blimmin' colander. Barely enough oxygen to last us till teatime. Then these things turned up. Ugly brutes, so they were. Demanded we surrender or they'd shoot us all into little bits, you see?'

'Right…' said the Doctor.

Vienna was now walking at his side, her brother following closely behind.

'Doctor?' she said. 'What's going to happen to our parents?'

The Doctor stopped walking and turned to face the children, crouching slightly so that he was level with them.

'Your parents are going to be fine. Trust me. I won't let anything happen to them. I just need to think of something…'

He straightened up and started walking again, his face scrunched up in concentration. Yes, he needed to think of something, but what? It was at times like this he missed having regular company. Not that he was helpless by himself, of course. No, the very idea was ridiculous. It was just helpful having another person to bounce ideas off.

There were Sontarans, and there were Rutans, and there were thousands of passengers and visitors. Was this one of those occasions when it might be enough to save just three lives?

He wouldn't have it. He'd seen far too many people suffer at the hands of creatures like the Sontarans and the Rutans, and had too many painful memories of their suffering. This, he decided right there and then, would be one of those occasions when he saved them all. He needed to speak to General Kade.

They were almost halfway to the door of the Doctor's hotel room when a figure appeared at the far end of the corridor. It was one of the Sontarans.

'Halt!' the creature bellowed, as it marched forward, its rifle aimed squarely at them.

'Hands up, kids, hands up,' said the Doctor, holding his hands in the air.

'Blimmin' surrender monkey,' said the Major. 'They'd have hanged us from the sat-com dish if we'd done this in my day.'

'Yes,' hissed the Doctor under his breath, 'but we're not *in* your day, are we? Plus, he's got a gun. We haven't.'

The Sontaran stopped marching when he was only a few steps away from them.

'You will come with me,' he snarled.

'Right,' said the Doctor. 'And where are we going, exactly?'

'That is no concern of yours,' said the Sontaran. 'You are in the custody of the Fourth Sontaran Intelligence Division, pending our investigations.'

'Only you see,' said the Doctor, 'I'm the Doctor. I was talking to your General Kade earlier. Lovely fella. And he said I was free to go, if I wanted to.'

The Sontaran turned now so that his back was facing the Major, Vienna, and Jake.

'Is that so?' he growled.

'Oh yeah,' said the Doctor. 'Me and General Kade, we're like *that*.' He held up his hand, his fingers crossed. 'Of course, if you want to go against the General's orders, I'm sure we can straighten this out when we get to wherever it is you're taking us…'

The Sontaran had no chance to reply for, in one sudden, violent move, the Major struck him from behind with his rolled-up newspaper. Dropping his gun to the ground and clutching at a narrow vent in the back of his neck with both hands, the Sontaran fell to his knees, wheezing and spluttering before he collapsed in a heap at their feet.

'Good shot!' said the Doctor. 'Where'd you learn that?'

'The Siege of the Hexion Gates,' said the Major, beaming. 'Never could stand those blimmin' Sontarans. Still… Quick pop on the back of the neck usually sorts 'em out. Probic vent, they call it. Hit one of 'em there and it's like kicking a chap in the you-know-whats.'

'Yes, Major,' said the Doctor. 'Now shall we go? Any time soon-ish? No hurry or anything, it's just he might wake up.'

'Oh. Yes. Of course,' said the Major. 'Lead on, Macduff, and all the rest of it.'

THIRTEEN

General Kade looked out through the glass dome of the Mayor's office at the black sky above and smiled. There would be medals upon his return to Sontar, of that he was sure. Medals and recognition. There were many in the Sontaran Empire who treated the Intelligence Division with disdain. Theirs was not a proper army, it was argued. Military Intelligence – espionage and the like – was a Rutan practice, ill-befitting a proud Sontaran warrior.

The Intelligence Division, for its part, had argued time and time again that in a war that they were losing thanks, partly, to the Rutans' cunning, they must match them in every aspect of warfare. Some in Sontaran High Command had spoken in favour of sending a whole fleet of battleships to destroy all life on every planet, moon and planetoid in this solar system. It was only Kade's eloquent counter-argument, delivered at the Senate, that had persuaded them otherwise. A simple search-and-destroy mission might eradicate all Rutan presence in that particular system, but there would be other worlds where the Rutans would have planted similar traps. Only by investigating the matter properly and interrogating the suspects would they gain any sort of advantage over the Rutans.

From the other side of the office there came the sound of a knocking at the door.

'Enter!' Kade snapped.

The door opened, and Colonel Sarg entered.

'Progress?' said Kade, turning to face his second-in-command.

'We have rounded up all but a handful of the humans,' Sarg replied. 'Unit B is ready to destroy the plants, sir, and the prisoners are being concentrated into the docking areas. We have control of the colony, sir.'

'Splendid,' said General Kade, balling one hand into a fist and then slapping it into the palm of the other.

'Permission to speak freely, sir?' said Sarg. He seemed agitated.

'Permission granted, Colonel Sarg.'

'Sir... I cannot help but think it would simplify matters if we were to exterminate all of the humans on this colony.'

Kade grunted, eyeing the Colonel in the patronising way that a teacher might look at their pupil.

'Colonel Sarg, you are no longer in the Battle Fleet. This is the *Intelligence* Division. We do things differently here. Our goal is victory, as it is the goal of the whole Sontaran Empire, but our methods are quite different. The human prisoners may seem like a hindrance to you, but to me, and indeed to the Intelligence Division, they are a vital asset in our war against the Rutans.'

'Yeah,' said a voice from the doorway. 'But war, ay? I mean… What *is* it good for, exactly?'

Both Sontarans turned to see the Doctor standing in the doorway.

'You?' said Kade. 'How did you get in here? There must be at least a dozen guards in the corridor.'

'Gift of the gab,' said the Doctor. 'And the gab is, after all, mightier than the gun. Anyway… Hello!'

Sarg lifted his rifle and aimed it at the Doctor.

'That will not be necessary,' said General Kade. 'Lower your weapon, Colonel Sarg. The Doctor and I will talk…'

'But…' Colonel Sarg began.

'In private,' Kade added.

Giving the Doctor a malevolent glare and hissing through clenched teeth, Colonel Sarg left the office, closing the door behind him.

Kade gestured towards the chair facing the Mayor's desk.

'Please,' he said. 'Sit.'

The Doctor nodded and, after crossing the room, sat down.

Kade remained standing, circling the desk slowly.

'You ask what war is good for, Doctor,' he said.

'Yeah,' said the Doctor. 'Well, actually it was Edwin Starr, originally. Or was it Sun Tzu? I can never remember…'

'Such a pointless question,' said Kade. 'Asking a Sontaran to explain the relevance of war is like asking a human to explain the relevance of music. War, Doctor, is our culture. It is why we exist. Furthermore, I fail to understand how one such as yourself can sit in judgement upon the Sontaran Empire.'

'What's *that* supposed to mean?' asked the Doctor.

'Are you not the last of your kind?' said Kade. 'Were your people and your world not destroyed in a calamitous war?'

'That's true,' said the Doctor.

'Then you understand what I am saying,' said Kade. 'Your people obliterated themselves in war. The people you care so passionately about, these *humans*, have spent every day of their existence fighting and killing one another, almost without exception. Our species are not so different. Time Lord, human, Sontaran – all dedicated to war. The only difference, Doctor, is that we Sontarans are proud to admit it. We understand our nature. The Time Lords operated under the pretence that they were a benevolent and superior race, and yet they still participated in the greatest act of self-annihilation the universe has ever known. The humans decorate their day-to-day existence with their superstitions, their *culture*, their love of so-called beauty, and yet they are little more than savages killing one another for personal gain and pleasure. Who, Doctor, are you to judge?'

'I'm not judging you.' The Doctor got up from his chair and faced Kade directly. 'I just want you to leave these people alone. You *and* the Rutans can wage your war elsewhere, but not here. Not with these people. Your war has nothing to do with the humans.'

'If they are human,' said Kade, 'they have nothing to fear. If they have become hosts for the parasitic Rutans, then I am afraid their fate is a little less fortunate, but it was not us who involved them, Doctor. Remember that.'

'And what will you do with them?' the Doctor asked. Kade smiled.

'We shan't kill them,' he said. 'Not yet, at least. They are worth infinitely more to the Intelligence Division alive than they are dead. When the Rutans first placed their trap in the atmosphere of this planet they imagined their hosts would be Sontarans. Fortunately for us the humans got here first. Humans are weak of body. Though the mind might be Rutan, the body is still quite human, and quite frail. The application of physical discomfort will soon result in many of the

Rutans giving up valuable information regarding their plans and whereabouts in this sector…'

'You're talking about torture,' said the Doctor.

'Well done,' said Kade. 'You're learning fast. We shall probably start with the younger prisoners. Their resistance to pain is so much weaker than the adults of the species, so I'm told…'

The Doctor stepped forward, raising his finger in anger, but still managing to hold himself back.

'If you harm just *one* of them…'

'You'll do what, exactly, Doctor? As warlike as your people may have been, I don't believe you have the nerve to do anything truly radical. You could have struck me then, but you didn't. If I were you, Doctor, I would leave while you still have the chance.'

The Doctor nodded, still shaking with anger. He turned his back on General Kade and walked towards the door.

As he left the Mayor's office, Kade called out, 'How does it feel, Doctor? How does it feel to have been outwitted by the Sontarans?'

FOURTEEN

They sat and waited in the darkness. Beyond the heavily bolted cupboard door they heard the sounds of the shop being torn apart: shelves ripped down, boxes overturned, the cash register being smashed into pieces and its contents jangling out onto the wooden floor.

They had sat and waited, silently, as the Sontarans came in and arrested Mrs Pemberton, dragging her out of the shop, screaming her husband's name to no avail.

Typical Sontarans, thought Mr Pemberton. They turned every stone but never thought to break down a cupboard door. If they had, they would have discovered him and Wallace, hiding in the shadows.

Only when there had been silence for several minutes did they step out of the cupboard and into the ruins of the shop, ensuring that they were out of view from the windows.

'We're receiving word from Mrs Carstairs,' said Mr Pemberton gravely. 'She and Mr Carstairs have been captured, but the children have not.'

'Really?' said Wallace. 'That's interesting.'

'Quite,' said Mr Pemberton. 'It appears the children have been rescued by the Doctor, and taken to his TARDIS.'

'The TARDIS? It's here? In the colony?'

'Well, of course. There's a chance they're still there. In the hotel.'

Wallace nodded thoughtfully.

'We understand our thinking?' said Mr Pemberton.

'We certainly do,' said Wallace. 'The Carstairs girl?'

'Exactly,' said Mr Pemberton. 'She's taken quite a fancy to young Wallace, hasn't she?'

'She has.'

'We could use that to our advantage, could we not?'

'Certainly.'

'A TARDIS. In our possession. It would enable us to leave this wretched colony and travel anywhere in the universe. Anywhere in *time*.'

'That would be agreeable.'

There was a long silence between the two of them. Somewhere out in Miramont Gardens they could hear the sound of Sontarans, marching, and so they both ducked down and hid behind the counter.

'Use the ducts,' said Mr Pemberton. 'They won't catch us in the ducts.'

'Where do you think they are?' said Vienna, pacing back and forth in the console room of the TARDIS.

'I dunno,' said Jake with a shrug. He was sat in one corner, idly going through the contents of an old crate he had found. All it contained, as far as he could make out, was old junk: a paperback novel, a glowing green ball and what looked like a frisbee.

'You sound like you don't care,' said Vienna.

Jake turned to his sister and scowled.

'I *do* care,' he said, 'but what can we do about it?'

'We should be out there,' his sister replied. 'We shouldn't be stuck in here waiting for the *Doctor* to come back. How do we even know he's coming back?'

'I trust him,' said Jake.

'Yeah? We don't even know him, not really. I mean… Who *is* he exactly? Look at this place! On the outside it's, like, *this* big.' She held her finger and thumb a fraction apart. 'But on the inside it's *huge*. That's just not normal. Where did he come from?'

'I don't know,' said Jake. 'But he said he'd look after us, and that he'd help Mum and Dad, and I trust him.'

'Yeah, well you would, wouldn't you? You're too busy daydreaming…'

'Now, now,' said the Major, stirring from a pensive silence. 'What use is a lot of brouhaha going to be?'

The twins looked at him in unison with exactly the same resentful frown.

'Listen,' said the Major, getting to his feet with a grunt. 'You can argue till you're both blue in the face, but it won't solve anything. Not now. This reminds me of the time we were stranded on one of the moons of Mercutio 14—'

'Yeah,' interrupted Jake. 'We've heard this one. You were clinging to the raft like limpets…'

'Quite right,' said the Major, regardless. 'Clinging to the raft like limpets. Ten of us.'

He stood between the twins now, at the edge of the hexagonal console in the centre of the room.

'There were arguments at first,' he said with a sad smile. 'Lots of bickering and whatnot. And the same thing occurred to all of us. It went unsaid, mind you. No need for us to get all girly and weepy in a situation like that, even the girls. We realised that there was no point. We had to stay focused on the task at hand, which was to get out of that dreadful swamp. When you're stuck in a situation like that, it's working together that will get you out, not shouting at one another like a load of hooligans.

'For what it's worth, I'm with young Jake, here. That Doctor seems to know a thing or two, and I trust him. Now if we just sit tight I'm sure it'll all be over in time for afternoon tea. Just you wait and see.'

***

The ventilation grill shuddered and shook and, with a final nudge from inside the air duct, came tumbling down into the hotel lobby.

With the grace and agility of a gymnast, Wallace lowered himself from the duct and dropped down behind the reception desk.

The coast was clear – no Sontarans anywhere to be seen – and so he was able to quite calmly go about the business of finding the spare key card for the Doctor's hotel room in a cupboard behind the desk, before making his way to the elevators.

He took the elevator up as far as the floor where Mrs Carstairs had told him telepathically the Doctor was staying. With every passing second, their power to communicate with one another by thought alone grew stronger.

Stepping out into the corridor he saw, halfway down it, a Sontaran soldier lying on its back, quite unconscious. Wallace made his way gingerly along the corridor and stepped over the body before approaching the door to the Doctor's hotel room.

He swiped the key card in the reader next to the door. A tiny light changed from red to green, and he entered the room.

It was empty.

There were the usual furnishings – the bed, a dressing table and chair, a smaller table with a lamp – but there was no TARDIS. In a state of increasing panic, Wallace sent his thoughts out across the colony to Mrs Carstairs, who could only reiterate that he *was* in the room where the TARDIS was being kept.

Wallace thought for a moment, and then, from the pocket of his apron, he produced a small plastic handset. He dialled a code and waited.

Inside the TARDIS there was a sudden, inexplicable ringing sound.

'What's that?' said the Major. 'Sounds like a blimmin' telephone. On a spaceship? Has the world gone mad?'

Jake looked at Vienna. The sound was coming from her, and his sister was blushing. With an embarrassed shrug, she reached into her pocket and produced a chatcom.

'You've got a chatcom?' said Jake. 'Do Mum and Dad know you've got one of those?'

Vienna shook her head.

'They don't?' Jake continued, and then, with a degree of pleasure, 'Oh, you are *so* dead when they find out. You are going to be grounded for, like, a *year* or something.'

Vienna scowled at him and answered the call.

'Wallace?' she said, half-excited and half-cautious. 'But where are you? They haven't? But…'

She paused, her expression gradually turning to one of concern.

'The Doctor, that man who was with us, he said you're one of *them*. You said those words… The same words as Mr Pemberton. The Doctor said that all these alien… *things*… He said they all say the same words. And *you* said them, Wallace. You did.'

There was a long pause. Jake could just about hear the muffled sound of Wallace at the other end of the line.

'Really?' said Vienna, smiling awkwardly. 'You mean that? You promise me you aren't?'

What *was* his sister talking about? What was Wallace saying to her? Jake was becoming increasingly frustrated that he couldn't hear both sides of the conversation.

'OK,' said Vienna. 'OK… We're in room 237. The Doctor moved his ship to keep us safe.'

'What are you doing?' Jake hissed, getting to his feet and lunging for the chatcom in his sister's hand.

'It's all right!' said Vienna, pulling it away, out of his reach. 'Wallace is OK. He's *not* one of them.'

'How do you know?'

'Because he promised me. He just heard Mr Pemberton saying that line, so he started saying it too. He's not one of those aliens that the Doctor was talking about. He's coming here now.'

'Oh, really?' said Jake. 'And who says so?'

'I do,' said Vienna. 'We can't just leave him out there. Those things might get him.'

Jake sneered and started walking around his sister with an exaggerated feminine wiggling of his hips.

'Oh,' he said, his voice whining and snide, 'I'm Vienna Carstairs and I can do what I want because my boyfriend wants to be in the spaceship with me so we can hug and kiss and cuddle. Mwah mwah mwah mwah mwah…'

Vienna lifted her hand to slap her brother's face, but they were interrupted by a knocking at the door.

'That'll be Wallace,' said Vienna. 'And if you say anything, I *swear*…'

'If you swear, I'll tell Mum you swore,' said Jake.

'I mean it,' said Vienna, crossing over to the main door. She opened it, and Wallace stepped in. He seemed to Jake more confident and more cheerful than he'd ever been inside Mr Pemberton's shop, especially considering what was going on in the colony outside.

When Wallace saw the Major he paused and laughed nervously.

'What's *he* doing here?'

'He's coming with us,' said Vienna. 'The Doctor's going to take us somewhere where it's safe. We *think*.'

'He *is*, actually,' said Jake. Looking over to the Major he saw that the old man was frowning.

'Wallace, is it?' the Major asked, getting up from where he sat and making his way slowly across the TARDIS.

'Yes…' Wallace replied, cagily.

The Major looked over to Jake once more, and shook his head.

'What is it?' asked Vienna. 'What's wrong? It's Wallace! You can *see* that it's him.'

'It's not,' said Jake. 'Look at him, Vienna… Look at him.'

Wallace's eyes darted from side to side, from Jake to the Major. His lips curled back in a sneer, baring his teeth, and he lifted up his hands like talons, balls of blinding white light glowing at his fingertips. He aimed his fingers at Jake and let out a terrifying howl, but before he could do another thing the Major had charged forward and wrestled him to the ground.

Together the old man and the boy rolled across the floor, cocooned in a shuddering ball of crackling energy, until Wallace broke free and got to his feet. The Major lay paralysed on the ground, his breath little more than a rattle.

'Wallace?' said Vienna, horrified. 'What have you done?'

'Oh, do hush,' snapped Wallace. 'With any luck we've killed him. Now where is the Doctor?'

Vienna shook her head, tears streaming down her cheeks.

Jake looked down at where the Major lay, still struggling for breath, and launched himself at Wallace, his hands reaching out as if he might strangle him. Wallace flicked his hand toward Jake with the slightest of gestures, and a thin bolt of zigzagging energy sent the younger boy reeling.

Wallace turned back to Vienna.

'Now,' he said, more coldly than before. 'Where. Is. The. Doctor?'

'I'm here,' said a voice from the doorway.

Wallace turned on his heels and saw the Doctor standing inside the TARDIS. He had closed the door silently behind him, and was now leaning against it.

'So,' said the Doctor, 'this is what's become of the Rutan Host after more than fifty thousand years of endless war, is it? Attacking old men and using teenage boys to do their dirty work for them?'

'What would you know of our kind?' said Wallace, leering at the Doctor.

'Oh, enough,' said the Doctor. 'Enough to know that you're more intelligent than the Sontarans, however pretentious they get. Enough to know that even when you're winning this war you never really *enjoy* it like they do, do you? I mean… The Sontarans… They love it. They *love* war. But the Rutans? No… You're different. So why do you do it?

'Do you know what I think? I think you do it out of boredom, and to make yourselves feel superior. There are billions – and I mean *billions* – of sentient life forms out there to pick a fight with, and you pick the *Sontarans*. It's kind of like playing chess with a lobster, really. OK… Not a *brilliant* analogy, but you get my drift. And yet you carry on doing it, because it makes you feel oh so important and clever.'

'Very insightful, Doctor,' said Wallace, lifting up his hand, the fingers splayed. 'And you may be right. Perhaps victory over the Sontarans will be too easy, in the end. Imagine how much greater our victory will be when we have killed the last of the Time Lords…'

He thrust his hand forward with a sudden jerk but nothing happened; no bolts of electricity, no flash of energy. Wallace looked down at his hand and frowned.

'Oh, that's another thing,' said the Doctor. 'I *also* know that this spore version of yourselves that you've engineered… It had to survive in Saturn's atmosphere for almost five centuries. To do *that*, it had to breathe ammonia.'

'But how…?' said Wallace. He was now looking weaker, his body hunching forward, his breaths getting shorter by the second.

'The smell,' said the Doctor. 'Noticed it when I first set foot on Chelsea 426. Not pleasant. The locals probably hadn't noticed it… You don't when you're around it all day. Like when somebody smokes. They can't smell the smoke, but everyone else can.

'The thing is, the TARDIS isn't a part of the colony, is it? The door's shut, and the air conditioning in this thing is second to none. Any whiff of something just a little bit nasty and it's straight out through the vents. You're running out of air.'

'What?' said Wallace, now struggling to breathe. 'But you can't… you can't do this…'

'Oh, I can,' said the Doctor, standing over Wallace as the young boy curled up on the floor, his mouth opening and closing like that of a fish out of water. 'I asked you to leave these people alone when I was talking to Mrs

Carstairs. You can remember that, can't you? Shared memories and all the rest of it. I asked you to leave, and you didn't.'

Vienna ran across the console room and knelt beside Wallace. She looked up at the Doctor, crying and red with anger.

'What are you doing to him?' she demanded. 'You're *killing* him…'

'I'm not,' said the Doctor. 'It's the Rutan spores. They're dying.'

Wallace looked up at the Doctor, his eyes narrowing malignantly, and laughed with what little breath he had.

'You'll regret this, Doctor,' he said. 'You *will* regret this.'

His eyes closed, and his head fell back onto the grilled metal floor of the TARDIS with a dull clank.

'What have you done?' Vienna cried. 'What have you done to him?'

The Doctor remained expressionless, walking around the console to where the Major lay clutching at his chest.

'I'm sorry,' said the Doctor. 'I'm so sorry.'

'Ah,' wheezed the Major. 'Don't mention it. Got hit worse than this in a dogfight over the Corinthian Archipelago. Can't say I'll pull through this time, though. How about the twins… Are they OK?'

'Yes,' said the Doctor, smiling weakly. 'They're fine.

Thanks to you.'

The Major smiled.

'That's good,' he said.

He closed his eyes and winced in pain.

'Well, Doctor, at least it wasn't one of them Sontarans that did me in, what? Little tyrants that they are with their funny little heads and their funny little ears.'

The Doctor laughed softly.

'That's the thing with little ears though,' said the Major. 'Only takes a little sound to deafen 'em.'

The Major held the Doctor's hand, squeezing it gently, and then he winked.

'What does that mean?' asked the Doctor. 'Major?'

'You'll work it out,' said the Major. 'Clever chap like yourself. Think I'll have a little nap, now. Feeling a little bushed, truth be told. Night, night, Doctor.'

The Major laughed and coughed one last time, and then his eyes closed and his arm fell limp at his side.

The Doctor ran one hand through his hair and let out a shuddering sigh. If only he had stayed with them, or returned from the Mayor's office just a few minutes earlier…

'I don't believe it!'

Vienna's voice interrupted his thoughts. The Doctor stood and, looking over the edge of the console, saw Wallace sitting upright, shaking his head as if he had been woken suddenly from a deep sleep.

'What happened?' he asked, coughing and spluttering.

'Where am I? Where's Mr Pemberton?'

'You were right,' said Vienna, looking up at the Doctor.

The Doctor nodded.

'See?' said Jake, smarmily. 'I told you we could trust him.'

The Doctor smiled at Jake, and then looked down at where the Major lay. He took a deep breath, and then faced the children once more.

'Right,' he said. 'Now all we need to do is sort out the rest of the Rutans, rescue your parents and send the Sontarans back to Sontar. Who's with me?'

Jake stuck his hand up in the air as high as he could reach. Vienna followed suit seconds later, which left only Wallace.

'I'm sorry,' he asked, 'but what's a Sontaran?'

FIFTEEN

It was the first time in two years that Mr Carstairs had seen the Western Docks. It was there that he and his family had first arrived, travelling from Earth on a liner bound for the Kuiper Belt. Their worldly, and indeed otherworldly, possessions had been packed away in a crate no more than a metre deep.

On arrival, they had all, even the children, been interviewed individually by check-in officials and made to present their transfer papers and the legal documents proving their authority to manage the Grand Hotel. The first few months had seen them treated very much as Newcomers by the other residents, but soon enough their neighbours and acquaintances had realised that they were Chelsea 426 people through and through.

Only the children had seemed to have any difficulty fitting in. Their peers on Chelsea 426 were so different from the children on Earth. Less boisterous, less mischievous, less noisy. They dressed less like teenagers and more like miniaturised versions of their parents and grandparents, not something either Jake or Vienna had ever done.

As a result, neither of them had made many friends, but that had caused Mr and Mrs Carstairs little concern. Having fewer acquaintances here on the colony meant they were less likely to get into trouble, not that there seemed to be much trouble for them to get into.

Mr Carstairs couldn't help but think of those first days on the colony as he and his wife were pushed into the loading bay at gunpoint by the Sontarans. The vast hall was crowded with familiar faces and strangers alike. Many of them were silent, sitting in small huddles looking lost and forlorn. Some were crying, their sobs echoing around the bay.

'You will wait here until further notice,' said one of the Sontarans.

When Mr Carstairs turned and glared at him aggressively, the Sontaran lifted his baton as a warning.

'Come along, dear,' said Mr Carstairs, holding his wife by the hand and leading her into the crowd.

He thought of the children now, travelling in that curious blue spaceship with a complete stranger. He hoped with every shred of emotion he had left that they were safe, and that the Doctor, whoever he might be, was true to his word.

As he led his wife further into the crowd, he felt her pull gently on his hand. She had stopped walking.

'What is it?' he asked.

'I won't be long,' she replied, gazing over at the far side of the loading bay.

'What do you mean?' he asked. 'Where are you going?'

'I won't be long,' she said once more, letting go of his hand and walking away, to where a small group of colony residents had gathered in one corner.

He was about to follow her when a voice said, 'Excuse me, but do you live here?'

Mr Carstairs turned to see a young couple, neither of them any older than 25. They were dressed in evening wear, though neither of them looked particularly used to wearing such clothes.

'Er, yes…' he replied, distantly.

'I'm Zack,' said the man, holding out his hand, which Mr Carstairs duly shook. 'And this is my girlf—'

He turned to the young woman at his side and they smiled at one another.

'This is my *wife*,' the young man corrected himself. 'Jenny.'

'Pleased… pleased to meet you…' said Mr Carstairs. 'I'm Mr Carstairs.'

The young couple frowned at him quizzically. Even

if they hadn't been dressed as if they had been dragged straight from one of the pleasure cruisers, Mr Carstairs could have guessed they were Newcomers just from the informality of their introduction.

'My name's Brian,' he said, after a pause. 'Brian Carstairs.'

'Well,' said Zack, 'pleased to meet you, Brian.'

Mr Carstairs couldn't remember the last time somebody had called him by his first name. Not even Mrs Carstairs had called him by his first name in such a very long time. It was always 'dear', or even 'Dad', particularly in front of the children.

'You were on one of the ships?' he asked, gesturing toward the enormous doors of the loading bay.

'Yeah,' said Jenny, still managing to smile. 'We're on our honeymoon.'

'Oh,' said Mr Carstairs. 'Oh… Congratulations.'

'Thanks.'

There was a moment's silence between them. Mr Carstairs had turned his attention once more to the corner of the loading bay, where his wife now stood, talking to the small group of colony residents. He recognised many of them but he couldn't say he knew all of them by name.

How could she know them?

'Do you think they'll let us go?' asked Zack.

Mr Carstairs turned back to face the young newlyweds.

'What's that?' he asked.

'These Sontarans. Do you think they'll let us go?'

He wasn't sure how much of an authority on the matter they expected him to be, but they were looking at him now with so much hope that he couldn't bear to shatter their illusions.

'Yes, I'm sure they will,' he replied. 'Just a few more hours, maybe, and then this will all be over.'

'I just want to go home,' said Jenny, her smile crumpling and a fresh tear rolling down one cheek.

Zack put his arms around her, holding her head to his chest and stroking her hair.

'You heard the man,' he said. 'It's gonna be fine.'

Suddenly the crowd beside them was split in two by a procession of Sontarans, marching toward them, their batons held in the air.

'You two!' one of them barked, pointing at Zack and Jenny with his baton. 'Come with us. You are to be *questioned*.'

'No!' sobbed Jenny. 'No, I don't want to go… No… Please, Zack… I don't want to go…'

Zack tried at first to hold them off, but it was no use. The Sontarans had them both turned and cuffed in a matter of seconds.

'Wait!' said Mr Carstairs, following them. 'Where are you taking them? What are you going to do to them?'

One of the Sontarans turned and held him back.

'That is no business of yours,' he growled.

The small group of Sontarans was nearing one of the exits when a voice cried out, 'Wait! Don't take them, take me!'

The unit stopped in its tracks, two of the soldiers holding Zack and Jenny still, and turned around to face the crowd. A man was pushing his way out past the others and into the open space between the crowd and the exits. It was Riley Smalls.

'Wait!' he said. 'I know where there are Rutans!'

The Sontarans looked at each other with expressions that Mr Carstairs could only read as puzzled. One of them let go of Jenny's shoulder.

'Is this true?' the unit leader barked at Smalls.

'Yes,' he replied. 'I know where there are Rutans. I can take you there. There are dozens of them.'

The unit leader turned to his group, eyeing Jenny and Zack in turn with a derisive sneer.

'Put them back with the others,' he said. 'We can interrogate them later.' He gestured at Smalls. 'Seize him.'

The cuffs were removed from Zack and Jenny's wrists, and they were pushed back towards the other residents and visitors.

The rest of the unit now surrounded Riley Smalls and walked him out through the doors. Only a handful of Sontarans stayed behind, each guarding an exit, but none in the crowd dared make a move.

Zack and Jenny walked back to where Mr Carstairs

was standing. Jenny was crying almost uncontrollably. Zack's jaw trembled, and he closed his eyes tight as if he were fighting back tears of his own.

'Are you OK?' said Mr Carstairs.

'Why is this happening to us?' asked Jenny. 'Why?'

They were in an elevator now, rising up above the Western Docks to a tier of exclusive luxury apartment pods.

'Where are you taking us, human?' asked one of the Sontarans.

Riley Smalls stood at the front of the elevator, facing the doors. He was glad they couldn't see his face, or his fear.

'My apartment,' he said, taking in a deep breath. 'There are Rutans there. They forced their way in, last night. They said it would be a good place to hide.'

The group leader grunted.

'And how do we know *you* aren't a Rutan?'

'I'm not,' said Smalls. 'But I'll take you to them. They're plotting against you as we speak.'

The Sontarans now murmured to one another in what he could only imagine was their equivalent of excited chattering. They seemed genuinely ecstatic at the prospect of engaging the Rutans in conflict.

Smalls took another deep breath, held it for a few seconds, then breathed out as slowly as he could, for fear that they might hear his nervousness.

The elevator stopped, and a synthesized human voice said, 'Level Five. Please confirm identity.'

Smalls placed his hand over a glowing screen above the elevator's control panel. A thin beam of light passed from top to bottom, the doors opened, and he led the Sontarans into his apartment.

It was a vast living space decorated sparsely with modern, minimalist furniture. There was a sunken seating area and a dining space, above which a circular, O-shaped fish tank was suspended from the ceiling. The apartment seemed almost too big for one person, yet there was nobody else to be seen.

'Where are they?' said the group leader, as they following him into the apartment, the doors closing behind them.

'I'll show you,' said Smalls.

He walked past the seating area, crossing over to the fish tank, stopping there for a moment to gaze up through its glass bottom at the fish inside.

'Hello there,' he said, tapping gently at the glass. 'Daddy's home. Not hungry yet, are we?'

Inside the tank, the fish darted around the artificial plants, weaving in and out of ceramic boots and miniature castles.

'Where *are* they?' the Sontaran grunted again, more forcefully this time.

'Oh yes,' said Smalls, turning to the Sontarans and smiling.

He left the dining area and made his way to the far wall, beside the large viewing window that gave him a view of the colony's enormous suspension disks and the clouds of Saturn stretching off into the distance. The wall itself was hidden behind two curtains, which Smalls set about opening, revealing a large round door, next to which there was a bright red lever.

'This way,' he said.

The Sontarans crossed the apartment, their guns charged and ready.

'What are you waiting for?' said the group leader. 'Open the door.'

Smalls nodded. The Sontaran's belligerent order had made this so much easier for him. There was no going back now.

He took a deep breath, swallowed, and pulled the lever.

All at once the lights in the room went out and were replaced with a dim red glow. Another synthesized voice spoke, coming to them from every corner of the apartment.

'Emergency exit activated. Emergency doors opening in ten…'

The Sontarans looked to one another, and then at Smalls.

'You betrayed us!' The group leader roared, as he and his men turned and bolted for the elevator doors.

'Nine… Eight… Seven… Six… Five…'

Together the soldiers tried to prise the doors apart, but it was no use. They were shut tight and airlocked.

'Four… Three… Two…'

The group leader turned to Smalls, and saw the human laughing, tears streaming from his eyes.

'One.'

With a thunderous crash, the circular emergency door was wrenched free and flung out into space like an enormous discus. The apartment was filled with a deafening roar as everything not bolted down was wrenched up and jettisoned with the force of a hurricane. Swinging back and forth on its chains, the fish tank shuddered and shook before breaking free, shattering as it caught the edge of the airlock, its contents flung out into the void like a shower of diamonds.

Smalls braced himself against the wall, deafened by the noise. The Sontarans clawed desperately at anything they could grasp, but it was no use. One by one they were picked up and thrown out through the airlock like rag dolls tossed aside by monstrous, unseen hands.

Smalls was losing strength. The air in the apartment was all but gone, the noise dying away into an unsettling silence, the temperature plunging lower and lower until his hands were numb and he felt even the moisture in his mouth begin to freeze. He had lost all consciousness when he too was finally launched out into the black and barren sky.

***

The Doctor couldn't help thinking it wasn't the best place to leave him, but it would have to do for now.

He drew the blanket up until it covered the Major's face, and for a moment he sat there, his head hung low. He wondered whether the Major had a family, and if so where they might be. Back on Earth, perhaps, or spread out across the galaxy on a dozen different colonies. It was hardly a fitting place to leave him, and hardly a fitting end to a life. He had to finish this, and soon.

He looked down at the Major's body one last time.

'Little ears,' he said, smiling sadly, 'and little noises. You're a genius, Major.'

He got up from the hotel bed and walked back into the TARDIS, where the three teenagers were now sat around the console. The high spirits following Wallace's recovery had now mellowed and been replaced by a sombre melancholy.

'So,' said Jake, looking up at the Doctor, 'what's the plan?'

The Doctor took a deep breath and smiled.

'Glad you asked,' he said, walking up to the console. 'Right… Now… Who knows who Francis Galton was?'

Jake, Vienna and Wallace frowned at him.

'Anybody? Anybody? No? Right… Francis Galton was the inventor of the dog whistle. You *must* know what a dog whistle is. No…?'

They shook their heads in unison.

'OK… A dog whistle is a whistle that only dogs can

hear. You see, a dog can hear anything from 16,000 to 22,000 Hertz. You must know what Hertz means… Right?'

'We kind of did it in school…' said Jake.

'*Molto bene!*' said the Doctor. 'OK… So dogs can hear anything up to 22,000 Hertz, but *humans*, you see, can only hear up to 20,000. Are you with me so far?'

They nodded, still looking at him with eyebrows raised in wonder as if they didn't really understand a word of it.

'So a *dog whistle*,' the Doctor continued, 'makes a sound that's *over* 20,000 Hertz. *Comprende?*'

'*Comprende*,' the teenagers mumbled.

'Great stuff! Now…' The Doctor started turning dials and flicking switches on the console, 'if I do *this*…'

Suddenly the TARDIS was filled with a single, near-deafeningly shrill note. Jake, Vienna and Wallace covered their ears with their hands, and then the noise ended as abruptly as it had begun.

'Horrible, wasn't it?' said the Doctor, grinning fiendishly.

'Ow!' said Vienna. 'Why did you do that?'

'*That*,' said the Doctor, 'was kind of like a human dog whistle. It's a frequency that drives humans *mad*! If I'd tweaked it just a teensy bit more you'd have all gone blind and keeled over.'

'You're mad!' said Wallace. 'Why would you want to do that?'

'OK, Wallace,' said the Doctor. 'I know this is all a bit new and weird for you, but you're going to have to bear with me on this one, OK? Right…'

He turned to the console once more, turning another dial and flicking another switch.

'Now how about *this*?'

The Doctor held out his hands as if he were demonstrating something sensational, but the TARDIS was almost silent.

'I can't hear anything,' said Jake.

'No,' said the Doctor. '*You* can't. But to a *Sontaran*…'

The teenagers looked at one another, still puzzled for a moment, until one by one the penny dropped and they looked back at him, grinning.

'You mean…?' said Vienna.

'Oh yes!' said the Doctor. 'The only thing is, I don't really fancy inviting all the Sontarans round for tea and biscuits just so I can deafen them.'

'So what can we do?' asked Jake.

'We,' said the Doctor, 'need to find somewhere that we can play that noise to the whole of the colony.'

He began pacing around the console and then, in a sudden fit of inspiration, darted out into the hotel room. The children followed, and found him staring down at the video screen in the corner of the room.

'Oh yes,' said the Doctor. 'Brilliant, just… brilliant.'

HURON PUBLIC LIBRARY
521 DAKOTA AVE S
HURON, SD 57350

SIXTEEN

The plants were now little more than a disintegrated mulch, a foot deep in places, that swamped the floor of the Oxygen Gardens. Sarg had only had to remind the unit that each plant contained millions and possibly billions of spores, each one capable of transforming another living being into the Rutan Host. Then, as they opened fire upon the plants with their rifles, they had taken to the task with relish.

Now the gardens were silent, the main chamber filled with the rancid odour of burnt vegetation. The Rutan plot had been foiled, their plans destroyed. All that was left to do was to execute those humans that the Rutans had already taken.

Sarg still harboured a desire to destroy the entire

colony. They could return to their ship and fire a single shot into the core of Chelsea 426 – a blast that would tear out the structure's heart and send it tumbling down into the tempestuous clouds of Saturn, leaving no survivors.

He was still frustrated with General Kade's unwillingness to listen. What kind of a Sontaran *was* he? Their mission so far had been far from Sarg's liking. Where was the combat that every Sontaran dreamed of? Where was the glory in taking prisoners? It made no sense to him.

He was about to call his unit together and take them back to the loading bays, when a lone soldier entered the main chamber.

'Colonel Sarg,' he said.

'Yes?'

'There has been an incident, sir. Unit 12… They were investigating possible Rutan activity above the Western Docks. It appears one of the humans, the man they called Smalls… He killed them, sir.'

Sarg walked towards the soldier, who in turn took a step back, as if he expected to be struck down.

'Killed?' said Sarg. 'What do you mean, "killed"?'

'He killed them, sir,' repeated the soldier. 'Blasted them out of an airlock. They're all gone, sir. All six of them.'

Sarg let out a terrifying roar, lifting up his rifle and firing it into the ceiling. There was a flash of light and then a shower of sparks, which rained down around them.

'Smalls, you say?' said Sarg.

'Yes, sir.'

'Was he Rutan?'

'No, sir. We don't think so.'

'Human?'

'Yes, sir.'

Sarg turned to the rest of his unit.

'Do you see?' he growled. 'This is what they are capable of, these *humans*. We should have killed them all when we had the chance. But Kade is a coward.'

The other soldiers looked at him now with surprise and the closest thing to fear that a Sontaran could express. Had the Colonel lost his mind? He was talking about a superior officer; the commander of their division.

'I am going to talk to General Kade,' said Sarg, walking now towards the exit of the main chamber, 'and I am going to demand that this time we leave and we destroy this den of vermin, once and for all.'

'So how do *you* know all about them, then?' asked Jake.

The four of them were crawling along one of the ventilation shafts that ran above Tunbridge Street, the Doctor in the lead with Jake and Vienna close behind, followed by Wallace.

'Who's that?' said the Doctor.

'These Rutans and Sontarans. How do you know all about them? I've never *heard* of them.'

'Met them before,' the Doctor replied. 'Far too many times. Mind you, once is enough. Thing is, they've been at war for fifty thousand years. You can go centuries with peace and quiet, and then it all flares up again. And they're forever fighting on somebody else's doorstep.'

'But *how* have you met them?' asked Jake. '*Where* did you meet them?'

'Oh, here and there,' said the Doctor. 'I think the first time I met the Sontarans was in Medieval England. Or was it Spain? It's all a bit weird…'

'Medieval England?' said Vienna in disbelief. 'Now I *know* you're making it all up.'

'Uh, hello…' said the Doctor. 'I'm the one with the little blue box that's bigger on the inside than it is on the outside. Is a trip to the Middle Ages all that weird? I mean, when you think about it? Really?'

'Uh… *yes*,' said Vienna. 'And that's another thing… *How* is it bigger on the inside than it is on the outside?'

'Right,' said the Doctor, 'here goes… You see, there are four dimensions that you're aware of, yes?'

'If you say so,' said Vienna.

'Well there *are*,' said the Doctor. 'Three in space, and one in time. But it's a bit more complicated than that. There are lots and lots of dimensions. It's a bit like having a box filled with lots and lots of little boxes.'

'A blue box?' said Jake.

'Well… It doesn't *have* to be blue,' the Doctor told him. 'Now, if you're holding the box you might not be aware of all the little boxes inside. But that doesn't mean they're not there… It's just that you can't see them. Well that's a little bit what dimensions are like.'

'Yes…' said Vienna, 'but the boxes inside the big box are still smaller than the big box.'

The Doctor sighed.

'You humans,' he said. 'You're one of the most endlessly fascinating and inventive species in the universe, but when it comes to something just a little bit confusing you're like toddlers sometimes. Every answer gets another question.'

'Well it's not *our* fault we're confused,' said Vienna. 'You're a very confusing man. And what do you mean, "you humans"?'

'Hush now,' said the Doctor. 'Jake… The map? We're coming to the end of Tunbridge Street. Which way to the studio?'

Kade had been expecting Colonel Sarg, even before one of his guards entered the Mayor's office to announce his arrival. Word had already reached him of Riley Smalls' moment of self-sacrifice. It was a curious act, but one he couldn't help but admire in some small way. It was utterly futile, of course, and had achieved nothing. Six Sontarans were lost, but they were mere foot soldiers. Nothing had changed.

When Sarg entered the office, Kade could immediately sense his anger.

'General, one of the humans has attacked us,' said Sarg.

'Yes,' said Kade, 'I am already aware of it.'

Sarg paused, seemingly surprised by this. 'Really?' he asked. 'And how do you think we should respond?'

'Respond?' said Kade. 'Colonel Sarg… We do not need to respond. We shall continue with our investigation as planned.'

'The *investigation*?' said Sarg. 'But sir… The situation here is volatile. If the *humans* are fighting back…'

'The *humans*?' said Kade with a dismissive snort. 'Their pitiful attempts at insurrection will do nothing to improve their situation.'

'We lost six soldiers, General…'

'I was aware of that, Sarg.' Kade crossed the office, tapping the palm of one hand with his baton. 'And how, Sarg, would *you* respond to this situation?' he asked, walking slowly in a circle around the Colonel. 'What would be *your* next move?'

Sarg shifted awkwardly, his gaze fixed on the ground.

'I would return to the ship,' he replied, 'and destroy the colony. Leave no survivors.'

'But of course,' said Kade. 'The Battle Fleet response. Destroy everything. Never mind the progress we are making. Never mind the evidence we have gathered.

Destroy everything, regardless of the greater good. And when, Colonel Sarg, our troops are ambushed by the Rutans in another system because of a plot almost identical to this one – a plot that comes as a surprise only because those who could have given us vital information were destroyed in your beloved inferno – what will you say then, Sarg?'

'We have been given no such information,' said Sarg, turning now to face the General. 'We have questioned many humans, using *all means necessary*, and not one of them has broken. Even those we strongly suspect of being Rutan have said *nothing*.'

'Then you have failed in your duty!' roared Kade. 'The humans are frail and weak and susceptible to pain, and yet they haven't broken? Question them *harder*. They *will* break.'

'They will not, *sir*.'

Kade stepped back from his second-in-command.

'Colonel Sarg, I do not like your tone,' he said.

'General, the men are behind me,' said Sarg. 'They are eager for war, and you have given them an *investigation*.'

'Really?' said Kade. 'So the men have your ear, now, do they? And they are behind *you*?'

'Yes, sir,' said Sarg.

Kade struck the palm of his hand with his baton once more, this time clenching his fingers around it.

'This is mutiny, then,' he said.

Sarg did not reply.

'Now that *is* a shame,' Kade continued. 'An immediate denial might have been just enough to spare your life. Your silence is a challenge, Colonel Sarg. A challenge to which there is only one solution.'

The television studio was exactly as the Sontarans had left it. The camera had been tipped over onto its side. Smalls' last speech lay scattered across his desk, half of it unread. On the floor, a sound technician's headphones lay next to an abandoned microphone.

'Wow,' said Wallace. 'It looks exactly like it does on TV.'

'Yes,' said the Doctor. 'Well it would do. What with it being a TV studio and everything.'

He walked across the studio towards a large wall, in the centre of which was a window. Through the window he could just about make out the dim glow of monitors, and a row of empty chairs.

'Bingo!' he said. 'Control room!'

To the side of the large window was a door. The Doctor tried the handle, but it was locked. He reached inside his jacket and drew out his sonic screwdriver.

'What's that?' asked Vienna.

'Sonic screwdriver,' the Doctor told her.

'A sonic *what*?'

'Sonic screwdriver. It's a screwdriver, only it's sonic.'

'And what does it do?' asked Vienna, still sounding faintly unimpressed.

'Watch,' said the Doctor, pointing the screwdriver at a keypad to the side of the door. The tip of the device suddenly lit up with a blue glow, and it emitted a shrill, high-pitched squeal. The keypad blinked into life and, with a soft clunk, the door was unlocked.

'Sonic screwdriver,' said the Doctor, holding it up to show the children. 'Just about the handiest thing in the universe. After a small towel. You can never go wrong with a small towel.'

Deep in the belly of Chelsea 426, the fusion candle blazed with the intensity of a sun, an intense column of white hot flame, channelled down towards the surface of the planet below.

Around the candle's flame were metal ramps and walkways forming bridges from one side of the cavernous space to the other, many of them passing within metres of the intense heat and light.

At either end of one such bridge were gathered the higher-ranking officers of the Fourth Sontaran Intelligence Division, while in its centre General Kade and Colonel Sarg faced one another.

Between them stood a third Sontaran, holding aloft two large metal staffs. The staffs were carved from end to end with intricate engravings; symbols and images as ancient as the Sontaran Empire itself.

'Colonel Sarg,' said the soldier. 'You have challenged the chain of command within the Fourth Sontaran

Intelligence Division, a challenge which amounts to mutiny. General Kade… You have countered Colonel Sarg's challenge by demanding a duel. As is the way of Sontar you must now fight… To the death.'

Kade and Sarg both nodded to the soldier, who handed them their weapons before walking to the far end of the metal bridge, leaving them alone at its centre. The General and the Colonel adopted battle stances and, but for the incessant throb of the fusion candle, the vast chamber fell silent.

Then, all at once, those gathered at either end of the bridge began to chant:

'Sontar-ha! Sontar-ha! Sontar-ha!'

Kade was first to act, swinging out the lower end of his staff in a sweeping arc that hit Sarg in his side, before lifting up the weapon to shield himself from Sarg's response. Sarg ducked down and thrust the end of his staff into the General's abdomen, sending him reeling back towards their audience.

Kade paused for a moment to gather his thoughts and then charged toward his second-in-command, swinging his staff this way and that so that it hacked through the air with a great whooping sound.

Sarg crouched again, lifting up his weapon, but Kade leapt up and flipped over in mid air, dropping down behind the Colonel and spinning on his heels with astonishing grace before striking Sarg in the back of his head.

Sarg lurched forward, clearly dazed by the blow, but recovered quickly, turning to face the General once more.

They met at the bridge's centre, staffs suddenly and violently locked together, each Sontaran pushing forward with all his strength.

Their audience continued to chant, even faster than before:

'Sontar-ha! Sontar-ha! Sontar-ha!'

Sarg seemed to have the upper hand, pushing Kade back against the bridge's barrier and bearing down on him with his full weight so that the General was now leaning precariously over the chasm into which the white flame of the fusion candle was channelled.

Sarg looked into the General's eyes. He sensed no fear in his commanding officer, but the General was beginning to tire, he could tell that much. Sarg was the younger of the two and, he felt, the stronger. It would take only one decisive blow to end this for good. Another violent shove, and he might just manage to push Kade over the edge of the bridge and send him tumbling down into the blazing inferno.

'Give up, Kade,' he said. 'It's over.'

Kade looked up at Sarg and, to Sarg's horror, laughed. With a forceful grunt, he pushed his own staff violently upwards, sending Sarg staggering back. For a moment they were separated, and the Sontarans at each end of the bridge fell silent.

This moment's pause was short-lived, for within seconds they had clashed once more, this time smashing their clubs together with such force that the noise of each collision very nearly drowned out the roar of the fusion candle. Kade delivered a blow to Sarg's chest. Sarg responded by slamming the end of his staff into Kade's stomach.

For a moment Sarg thought he had beaten him; the General was now doubled over, clutching his stomach and wincing in pain.

But Sarg was wrong.

With a look of fierce malevolence, Kade stood straight and then, with a speed that took the younger Sontaran by surprise, charged forward with an almighty roar.

In one sudden move, he swung his staff around in a dizzying arc, tearing Sarg's weapon from his hands and sending it spinning, end over end, into the blinding light of the fusion candle, where it was vaporised in a nanosecond.

Sarg held up his hands to defend himself, but it was no use. Kade was upon him at once, beating him to the ground. The General threw his weapon to the floor and with terrifying strength lifted Sarg up into the air until his feet left the ground.

Sarg looked down at Kade but, before he could plan his next move, the General had turned and, with one final, triumphant bellow, thrown him over the edge of the bridge.

As Colonel Sarg merged with the light and the heat of the fusion candle, he almost instantaneously vanished, his last, desperate scream cut off as suddenly as it had begun.

Kade now stood alone at the centre of the bridge. At either end those gathered were now silent, looking upon the General with dumbstruck awe.

The soldier who had handed them their weapons walked out once more and, standing at the General's side, shouted, 'General Kade is victorious! All hail General Kade!'

'All hail General Kade!' cried the Sontarans. 'Sontar-ha! Sontar-ha! Sontar-ha!'

'OK,' said the Doctor, flicking switches and pressing buttons. One by one the screens of the control room were turned on. 'Now if I just do this… And… *this*…'

On one monitor they saw the video screens of Miramont Gardens switch from the logo of *The Smalls Agenda* to a dazzling blue.

'Right,' said the Doctor, leaning in towards a microphone in the centre of the control panel. 'Testing testing… One-two, one-two…'

Beyond the studio they heard his voice echoing through the streets and thoroughfares of Chelsea 426. The Doctor laughed.

'Ha!' he said. 'I've always wanted to do that. Ever since Woodstock. Now… If I just do *this*…'

He lifted his sonic screwdriver to the microphone. Once again it was lit up blue, but this time none of the teenagers could hear a thing.

'Watch the screens, kids,' said the Doctor. 'This is gonna be good.'

SEVENTEEN

It happened quite suddenly. One moment the Sontarans guarding each exit to the loading bay were standing there, stoic and immovable; the next they were on their knees, their hands clasping their ears.

None of the prisoners could hear a thing, and yet the Sontarans appeared to have been deafened by some almighty noise. The only thing the humans in the loading bay *had* heard was a strange voice saying the words, 'One-two... one-two...'

And now this.

At first all they could do was look at one another in confusion. Then, gradually, the humans began to talk; a low murmuring that increased in volume; questions overlapping questions.

'What's happening?' asked Jenny, holding her husband by the arm.

'I don't know…'

'Are they dying?'

'I don't think so… I don't know.'

Mr Carstairs was one of the first to step forward, leaving the main group. He walked slowly towards one of the Sontaran guards, his heart pounding in his chest, waiting for the moment when the guard would stand and come at him with his baton or rifle, but it didn't happen. Closer and closer he got, but the guard stayed down, his hands over his ears. As Mr Carstairs got closer still, he heard that the creature was making an agonised, strangulated mewling sound in the back of its throat.

'What is it?' asked Mr Carstairs. 'What's happening to you?'

The Sontaran looked up at him, and their eyes met. The soldier could barely contain his anger, grinding and gnashing his teeth, but he was powerless.

Behind Mr Carstairs, more of the prisoners now came forward; tentatively at first, but gradually increasing in number, until the stricken guards were surrounded.

Mr Carstairs looked over to the other side of the loading bay and saw his wife and a small group of residents making their way towards one of the exits. He broke free of the throng and ran to where his wife and the others had now gathered at the door.

'Bess!' he said. 'Where are you going?'

'We're leaving,' said Mrs Carstairs quite calmly.

'Leaving?' said Mr Carstairs. 'But where? We don't know what's happening yet.'

It was now that he noticed that one of the residents at the exit was Mr Pemberton.

The shopkeeper turned to him with a menacing glare.

'We are leaving,' he said.

Mr Pemberton turned to the locked door and reached out towards its security panel. There was a flash of light, and tiny bolts of electricity shot out from his finger tips, causing the security panel to fizz and spark. The door slid open.

'What…?' said Mr Carstairs. 'But how did you *do* that? What did you just do?'

'We are leaving,' said Mrs Carstairs, and together she and the others walked out through the door and made their way into the colony.

After a moment's pause, Mr Carstairs followed.

All around him he saw warriors on their knees, wailing in agony. He had only enjoyed a moment's glory when it happened – that low rumbling, a sound that instantly rendered every Sontaran immobile. Every Sontaran except for Kade.

He clawed his way along the ground on his hands and knees towards one end of the bridge, where soldiers lay rolling around in agony. He could hardly see; his vision was blurring and warping, coloured dots dancing before his eyes.

There was only one person in the colony who could have done this; one person who could have thought of a weakness and exploited it. The Doctor.

However, Kade's thoughts were not of revenge. He was focused solely on stopping that sound, that crippling sound that seemed to tear through every fibre of his body.

Using what little strength he had left, Kade dragged himself onto the wide metal platform and tore the rifle from the grasp of one of his soldiers. He looked up at the edges of the chamber and saw the large speakers from which the sound came. His hands still shaking and his head still filled with noise, he took aim and fired.

One of the speakers exploded with a shower of sparks. He took aim at another, and fired again. He blasted the speakers apart, one by one, until, as suddenly as it had started, the noise stopped.

The gathered Sontarans ceased their wailing and got to their feet. Kade surveyed his soldiers with disgust, then made his way to the chamber's exit. There was only one place that noise could have come from, one place where the Doctor could be. He had offered the Doctor a means to escape. The Doctor hadn't listened.

He would have nobody to blame for his fate but himself.

***

'Oh… Not good,' said the Doctor.

'What's not good?' asked Jake.

The bank of monitors in the control room now showed a number of views of the colony. In one dimly lit corridor they saw General Kade, leading a procession of Sontarans away from the fusion candle. As they came to each new section of corridor, the General would take aim and blast apart the source of the noise that had deafened them.

'Looks like the General's a bit miffed,' said the Doctor. 'Though that *might* be an understatement. I think he's coming this way.'

Elsewhere in the colony, on walkways that had been deserted, passengers and residents now ran from the loading bays and out into the streets.

'Well,' said the Doctor, 'at least it *kind of* worked.'

'So what do we do now?' asked Wallace.

'Right,' said the Doctor. 'First we have to get out of here before the General turns up. *Then* we have to get rid of all the ammonia. I mean, for one thing, it doesn't smell very nice, and for another, if we get rid of the ammonia we get rid of the Rutans.'

He paused, and then smiled.

'Rid of the Rutans. They're a very alliterative race, aren't they? Root out the Rutans… Rid of the Rutans… Around the ragged rock the ragged Rutan ran…'

'Doctor,' said Vienna impatiently. 'The Sontarans…? Are coming this way…?'

'Oh, yeah,' said the Doctor, leaving the control room. 'This way, kids.'

'Where are we going?' asked Jake.

'The Oxygen Gardens.'

'Hang on,' said Jake. 'That's where those plants are. The evil ones, I mean.'

'That's true,' said the Doctor. 'Not trying to tell me you're scared of a few overgrown dandelions, are you?'

Jake huffed, as if he found the Doctor's words insulting.

'I didn't *say* I was scared of dandelions,' he said.

'Mm,' said the Doctor, with mock sympathy. 'Petrified by pansies?'

'No!' said Jake. 'But those plants… they're different.'

'Yeah,' said the Doctor. 'But this time they'll have you guys to contend with, won't they?'

The teenagers looked at one another, puzzled, and then back at the Doctor.

'Oh, come on!' said the Doctor. 'What's with the glum faces? In an hour's time, you three will have defeated an alien race and saved the colony. And all in time for tea.'

Jake, Vienna and Wallace laughed.

'You're serious?' asked Vienna.

'Oh yes,' said the Doctor.

'How can you be so sure?'

'Because I'm the Doctor.'

'That's it? Because you're the Doctor?'

The Doctor nodded, standing now beside the

opening in the ventilation shaft through which they'd entered the studio.

'Women and children first,' he said, beaming.

'You're weird,' said Vienna, laughing as she climbed into the vent, followed quickly by Jake and Wallace.

'Oh yes,' said the Doctor, checking that the coast was clear before joining them. 'But I'm also right.'

'Where are you going?' asked Mr Carstairs, though he realised the question was futile. They wouldn't answer.

The others were several paces ahead, walking with such speed and purpose that he struggled to keep up.

'I really think we should have stayed back in the Docks,' he continued, instantly aware of how hopeless and pathetic he sounded. 'Safety in numbers and all the rest of it.'

They came to the end of the narrow tunnel linking the Western Docks with Miramont Gardens. As they descended the metal staircase into the square itself they saw, lined up shoulder to shoulder on the other side, the Sontarans.

'Halt!' barked the unit's group leader.

The small group of residents stopped in their tracks.

'Return to the Docks at once!' The Sontaran continued. 'You are prisoners of the Fourth Sontaran Intelligence Division!'

Mr Pemberton stepped forward, walking calmly towards the Sontarans without a trace of fear.

'Halt!' the group leader shouted once more, but either Mr Pemberton didn't hear him, or he didn't care. He walked straight out into the centre of the square and stood alone before the wall of Sontaran soldiers.

'Sontarans, prepare weapons!' bellowed the group leader.

The long line of Sontarans lifted their rifles and took aim.

Mr Carstairs pushed past the others in the group and held his wife by the arm.

'Bess… Come on, Bess, we need to go back. They have *guns*, Bess…'

Mrs Carstairs did not respond. She, and the others in the group, were staring blankly ahead at the Sontarans.

'Sontarans… Fire!'

As the muzzles of the Sontaran rifles flared red, Mr Pemberton held up the palm of his hand. The laser beams came forth in an almost blinding arc but exploded in mid air before they had a chance to reach their targets.

Mr Pemberton's hand curled up into a fist which he threw forward, as if punching an invisible foe. One by one, the Sontarans' rifles fizzed and crackled in their hands, sparks jumping out of each weapon's inner mechanisms.

The Sontarans dropped their guns to the ground and lifted up their batons. With an almighty battle cry they charged forward, but the residents, with the exception of Mr Carstairs, stayed exactly where they were, unflinching.

As one, they repeated Mr Pemberton's gesture, lifting up the palms of their hands and then flinging them forward. A visible wave of energy pulsed from one side of the square to the other, knocking back the Sontarans with the force of a hurricane.

As the noise died down, the Sontarans got to their feet. They recovered their batons and once again charged forward, but had advanced by no more than three paces when a second wave of energy, more powerful than the last, struck them to the ground like skittles.

Mr Carstairs looked from the fallen Sontarans to the residents. He could scarcely believe what he was seeing, but had little time to take it in. He looked at the complete lack of emotion in his wife's expression and knew right then that everything the Doctor had told him was true. He let out a brief and desperate gasp of horror, as sure as he could be that he'd lost his wife, his Bess, for good.

As Mr Carstairs collapsed to his knees and wept, and the Sontarans got to their feet once more, Mr Pemberton, Mrs Carstairs and the others moved forward, marching silently toward their enemy with terrifying intent.

EIGHTEEN

The smell of burnt plants was overpowering. Only a few hours earlier, the Doctor, Jake and Vienna had stood in gardens extravagantly decorated for the Flower Show; the towering plants rising up from their flowerbeds, enormous banners welcoming the guests, and the stage on the far side flanked by enormous video screens.

Now they were in ruins. The video screens were shattered, the banners hanging in shreds, and the plants were scorched and pulped.

'It stinks!' said Jake.

'Yeah,' said the Doctor, sniffing the air and grimacing. 'Looks like the Sontarans got here before us. You don't need to worry about the dandelions after all, Jake.'

'I told you, I'm *not* scared of dandelions.'

'Course not.' The Doctor looked at Jake with a cheeky grin and winked.

They walked across the main chamber, doing their best to step around the vile black sludge that covered the whole floor from one end of the room to the other.

'Looks like the Flower Show's over, then,' said Wallace, looking down at the smouldering flowerbeds.

'Yeah, I reckon,' said the Doctor. 'Can't say they'll be having another one next year…'

When they came to the corridor on the other side of the gardens, the Doctor stopped to read a large board fixed to one of the walls.

'Right,' he said. 'Research centre… Labs… Ah! There it is! Climate Control. Come on, kids. Onwards and upwards.'

They walked a little further down the corridor until they came to a darkened staircase.

'I'm not going up *there*,' said Vienna.

'Oh, all right, then,' said the Doctor. 'Me, Jake and Wallace here will go up, and you can stay down here with all the evil alien plants. Sound like a plan?'

'But the plants are *dead*, Doctor…'

'Yeah, but that's the thing with evil alien plants, y'see. They might *look* dead, but…'

'All right, all right, I'll go,' said Vienna, rolling her eyes.

***

General Kade and his most senior officers stood in the deserted television studio. The control room fizzed and sparked in the aftermath of an assault that had lasted seconds. The source of that terrible sound had been destroyed, but there was no sign of the Doctor.

Kade was about to order their return to the civic centre, in preparation for their next move, when the broken studio door creaked open and a soldier entered the room.

'General Kade,' he said. 'The Rutans… They're free, sir.'

'I thought as much,' said Kade. 'Have you engaged with them, soldier? In combat?'

'We did, sir, but they were too strong. They have their powers, sir. Our weapons are no match for them—'

'No match?' Kade bellowed. 'What do you mean, no match?'

'Our rifles, sir. They exploded in our hands. There were only a few of them, but everything we tried failed.'

'Failure is not the way of Sontar!' roared Kade.

'But, sir…'

The General lifted up his baton, high above the soldier's head, but did not strike. If their rifles had failed and the Rutans were now in full possession of their powers what *could* they do?

There was only one option left.

***

Mr Carstairs followed them, though for the life of him he wasn't sure why.

He had seen his wife's face as she marched towards the Sontarans, and he had seen her slaughter them without mercy. Any glimmer of hope he'd had was evaporated in that moment.

He had wondered whether he should return to the Docks, but he couldn't go back. Not without her. He had to remind himself that it *wasn't* her; it wasn't his wife. But if it wasn't his wife, who was it? *What* was it? If he returned to the Docks, what would he do when he got there?

There were so many questions and so few answers. Nothing made sense any more, and so he followed them. He followed them across Miramont Gardens, as the Sontarans beat a hasty retreat, and down the deserted thoroughfares towards the botanical gardens.

Why were they going there? What did they expect to find when they got there? More and more questions, with still fewer answers.

From distant pods in the colony he heard the sounds of battle: short electric bursts of rifle fire often followed, very quickly, by the boom of another shockwave. His wife, Mr Pemberton and the others were not the only ones, it seemed.

A platoon of Sontarans ran past them, perhaps gathering themselves for a counter-attack, but paid them no heed. They might as well have been invisible.

When they eventually got to the Oxygen Gardens they found the entire area filled with acrid smoke. Mr Carstairs sensed that they were growing increasingly anxious. At least he took it to be anxiety; their expressions were so impassive they were almost impossible to read. They certainly seemed restless and, on entering the main chamber and discovering the plants there ruined, they collectively gasped.

'Destroyed,' said Mr Pemberton, his voice low and filled with threat. 'All of them destroyed.'

'The Sontarans…' said Mrs Carstairs.

'What's happening?' asked Vienna, peering over the Doctor's shoulder.

'Nothing,' said the Doctor, putting on his glasses and squinting at the screen.

'What do you mean, "nothing"?'

'They've locked this thing. Some sort of code. Typical Rutans. If the Sontarans had done this their password would have been "Sontar", I can guarantee it. But the Rutans… They're crafty little gelatinous blobs when they want to be.'

The colony's Climate Control Centre was a small room above the Oxygen Gardens, a room filled with buttons, blinking lights, and dozens of monitors, each showing a different view of Chelsea 426.

As the Doctor toiled at one of the computers and Vienna watched him, Jake and Wallace looked up at the large wall of video screens, wide-eyed with wonder.

'The Sontarans are running away...' said Jake. 'What's happening?'

'That'll be the Rutans,' said the Doctor. 'No more messing about for them. I've given them a golden opportunity. The Sontarans are switching to Plan B, most likely, whatever Plan B is. Now how do I unlock this thing?'

Vienna leaned in closer to the screen.

'Have you tried bypassing the file membrane with a logan key?'

The Doctor turned to her and took off his glasses.

'What?'

'The file membrane. If you upload a logan key from the user matrix, you can bypass the file membrane.'

'Are you still speaking English?'

Vienna rolled her eyes.

'Here,' she said. 'Let me do it.'

Vienna nudged the Doctor out of the way and began tapping at keys and moving objects around the touch-screen with her fingertips.

'What are you doing?' asked the Doctor.

'Like I *said*, I'm uploading a logan key so that we can bypass the file membrane.'

'Wait,' said the Doctor. 'Wait a minute. How come I didn't know how to do that?'

'You don't know how to do this?'

'No!'

Vienna laughed.

'It's something you learn in school. When you're, like, 8 or something. I mean, obviously I'm not meant to be doing it on *this* computer, and normally there'd be people here to *stop* me doing this sort of thing on *this* computer, but… you know… they're not here. So I'm doing it.'

'But how come I don't know how to do that?'

'It's probably because you're old. Or because you're probably an alien. Or just because you're weird.'

'But I know everything!'

'Well,' said Vienna, 'clearly you don't.'

She stepped back from the computer.

'There,' she said. 'All yours.'

The Doctor nodded, still frowning, and put his glasses back on. Sure enough, the Climate Control Centre was now at his command. Laughing gently to himself, he went about turning on the filtration units that were spread throughout the colony, instructing them to remove every last trace of ammonia from Chelsea 426.

'Vienna!' shouted Jake, still facing the wall of video screens.

Vienna turned from the Doctor and the console to her brother. He was pointing up at one particular screen showing an image of the Oxygen Gardens below.

She left the Doctor at his work and, joining her brother, saw that there were people down there. Not just people. Their parents.

'Mum!' she said. 'Dad!'

Not thinking twice, Vienna and Jake ran from the Climate Control Centre, with Wallace following close behind. As the door closed behind them with a thud, the Doctor looked up from his computer and found himself alone. He looked over at the wall of monitors and saw, in the gardens, Mr and Mrs Carstairs and the other residents.

'Oh no,' he murmured. 'Really bad idea.'

Hitting one last button on the console, he ran and followed them down the stairs and back into the gardens.

Jake and Vienna were already there, and they ran to their mother, heedless of the black ooze beneath their feet, their arms open and ready to embrace her.

Mrs Carstairs, in return, looked upon her children with an icy glare.

Jake and Vienna stopped running, and their arms fell to their sides.

'Mum?' said Jake.

Seeing his children, Mr Carstairs came forward. He smiled, but they could see a sadness in his eyes. Their father looked scared.

'Jake, Vienna,' he said. 'Stay there. Please.'

'Dad?' said Vienna. 'What's happening, Dad?'

Behind them the Doctor came skidding to a halt, almost losing his balance as his feet slid in the black sludge.

'The Doctor,' said Mrs Carstairs with a venomous smile.

'It's over,' said the Doctor. 'You must know what happened to Wallace. He's not one of you any more.'

'Then we must leave,' said Mrs Carstairs, still smiling. 'Perhaps, Doctor, you would be so kind as to aid our escape with that TARDIS of yours.'

'I can't do that,' said the Doctor.

Mrs Carstairs' expression changed quite suddenly from a smile to a bestial grimace and she lunged forward, seizing Vienna by the throat.

'Really, Doctor?' she sneered. 'Even if there is a human life at stake?'

'Let her go,' said the Doctor. 'Let her go now.'

Mr Carstairs leapt forward, reaching out towards his wife and daughter in anguish, but was knocked back as if he had run into a force field.

'This, then, is the weakness of the Time Lord,' said Mrs Carstairs, the menacing smile returning to her lips. 'For all your cunning, you cannot bear to see another living creature suffer. A saving grace to some species, Doctor, but not to us. Take us to the TARDIS and away from this colony and we may just spare your life and the lives of the humans.'

'Oh, I don't think so,' said the Doctor, only now it was he who smiled.

'Really, Doctor?' said Mrs Carstairs. 'You seem very sure of yourself.'

The Doctor craned his head back and breathed in deeply through his nose.

'Ah,' he said, still smiling. 'Nothing like the sweet smell of fresh air, is there?'

'What do you mean?' asked Mrs Carstairs.

'Smell it,' said the Doctor. 'Nitrogen, oxygen, a pinch of argon, a soupçon of carbon dioxide and a squeeze of H_2O. But no ammonia. Mmm… Lovely, isn't it?'

Mrs Carstairs tightened her grip on Vienna's throat.

'No,' she snarled. 'You can't have. The system was locked.'

'Oh yes,' said the Doctor. 'It was. And to be honest, if I'd been here on my own I wouldn't have stood a chance. Thankfully that daughter of yours has a brain the size of Jupiter.'

He looked at Vienna, and winked, before returning his gaze to Mrs Carstairs. His smile now faded.

'Only she's not *your* daughter,' he continued. 'She's Mrs Carstairs' daughter. It's over.'

Mrs Carstairs let go of the young girl and threw her forward, staggering back towards the rest of the group. Her movements were clumsy and awkward, her hands bunching up like talons.

The others were now doubled over, each of them gasping for air as if there were none to breathe, clutching at their throats and their chests.

'What's happening?' said Mr Carstairs, looking up at the Doctor. 'What have you done to them?'

Vienna and Jake ran to their father's side.

'It's OK, Dad,' said Vienna. 'Trust me. It's OK.'

One by one, Mrs Carstairs, Mr Pemberton and the others fell to the ground, rolling around in the dark slime, twitching and shuddering until all at once they were silent and still.

'You've killed them!' said Mr Carstairs, falling at his wife's side, stricken with grief. 'You've killed my wife…'

The Doctor waited. Though he would never say as much, a small part of him was worried that Mr Carstairs might be right. What if the Rutan spores were so enmeshed with the humans' DNA that the sudden starvation of ammonia *could* kill them? What if he had made a mistake? What if, right now, there were humans collapsing and dying all around the colony? His two hearts began to beat a little faster, and he closed his eyes, fearing the very worst.

'Brian?'

The Doctor opened his eyes once more to see Mrs Carstairs, sitting upright, cradled in her husband's arms.

'What happened?' asked Mrs Carstairs, bewildered. 'Where are we?'

All around them the other residents were now waking, many of them looking at the vile sediment covering their clothes with disgust.

Mr Carstairs helped his wife to her feet and then

threw his arms around her, kissing her and stroking her hair and holding her as tightly as he could. Jake and Vienna embraced their parents, so that the four of them now stood together, laughing and crying.

Their moment of joy and relief was interrupted, very suddenly, by the sound of marching feet.

The Doctor turned and saw General Kade emerging from the darkness of one of the corridors, flanked by two of his soldiers. The General marched out into the gardens, a glass dome containing a single bright blue flower under one arm, and approached the Doctor.

'Ah,' said Kade. 'The Doctor. I suppose you are happy that you have jeopardised our mission and handed victory to the Rutans? Was that all a part of your plan?'

'Actually,' said the Doctor, 'far from it. You see—'

'Silence!' said Kade. 'Once again you assume that you have bested us, Doctor, but I can assure you that is not the case. Sontarans... Prepare weapons.'

The two Sontaran soldiers lifted their rifles and aimed them squarely at the Doctor.

'No,' said the Doctor. 'No no no... Wait... You see...'

The General took a deep breath, ready to give the order to fire but, before he could speak, Mr Carstairs had stepped forward, between the Sontarans and the Doctor.

Unnoticed by either, Mr Carstairs took a deep breath. He hadn't thought this through properly; it was a decision forged in a moment of sheer panic, an idea that had come to him so suddenly he hadn't given himself proper time to consider just how ridiculous it might be.

Remaining perfectly silent, his eyes open but glazed over, his face without expression, he lifted up his open hand, just as Mr Pemberton, his wife and the others had done in Miramont Gardens.

'General Kade,' said one of the Sontarans with a gasp. 'He's one of *them*, sir…'

'A Rutan…?' said Kade, staring at Mr Carstairs aghast.

He turned to his guards and ordered them to lower their weapons with a single gesture of his hand. The Sontarans followed the command.

General Kade turned back to the Doctor.

'Very well. If you wish to pick a side in this war, Doctor, so be it. It will not change your predicament.'

Still dazed by what Mr Carstairs had done, the Doctor gathered his thoughts and walked towards General Kade.

'Oh yeah?' he asked. 'And what predicament would that be, then?'

Kade laughed callously.

'A subtle manoeuvring of the flotation panels and an adjustment to the coordinates, Doctor. You have heard, perhaps, of that which the humans call the Great White Spot?'

His brow furrowing with growing concern, the Doctor nodded.

'A storm larger than the Earth itself,' said Kade, still smiling. 'A storm into which this colony, and all of its inhabitants, will soon be drawn and dashed into atoms. So, you see, this victory is ours, Doctor. You cannot hope to save all of the humans in that machine of yours. You must leave them all to die or stay and join them in their fate. I bid you farewell, Doctor. It has been an honour.'

The General reached up to the collar of his armoured suit and pressed a small button.

Within a split second, the three Sontarans were engulfed in a flare of bright red light, and in the blinking of an eye they were gone.

The Doctor turned to Mr Carstairs.

'Way to go, Mr C!' he shouted, holding up his hand for a 'high five' which never came.

The recovering residents were still brushing the noxious mulch from their clothes.

'What was all that about?' asked Mr Pemberton.

'I'm not sure,' said Mr Carstairs, smiling bashfully. 'I don't know what came over me, really.'

'Well it did the trick!' said the Doctor. 'Only problem now is, we're about to crash into one of the biggest storms in the solar system. We need to get to the Docks. Come on! *Allons-y!*'

As the Doctor led the Carstairs family and the others

out of the botanical gardens, Mrs Carstairs turned to her husband.

'I'm sorry, dear,' she said, 'but do you have the faintest idea what's going on?'

NINETEEN

From the moment the sirens started there was chaos. It was a siren the residents knew well from the colony's monthly drills. Only this was not a drill.

They were evacuating Chelsea 426.

Led by the Doctor, Jake, Vienna and their parents ran from the Oxygen Gardens to the Western Docks. Every thoroughfare and corridor was clogged with residents fleeing in every direction, some of them dragging hastily packed suitcases or clutching framed photographs under their arms. When they got to the loading bays at the Western Docks, they found the placed swamped with panicking crowds of residents and Newcomers alike.

'Humans,' the Doctor muttered under his breath.

'Inventors of the queue, but they hear a siren and all hell breaks loose.'

As he made his way through the teaming masses with the children and their parents close in tow, the Doctor came eventually to Mayor Sedgefield, who was talking to Captain Thomas.

'Please, man… You must have room on that ship of yours,' the Mayor begged.

'I'm telling you, Mr Mayor, we have neither the supplies to feed extra passengers nor the oxygen for them to breathe. You must have life rafts?'

'Not enough,' the Mayor cried, his face a mask of frustration. 'The women and children? Surely you could begin taking them on board…'

The Captain shook his head forcefully.

'I'm sorry, but there simply isn't enough time to start processing your residents as well as our passengers.'

In one last desperate gesture the Mayor reached forward, grabbing Thomas by his lapels.

'Do you want us all to die? Please… I am *begging* you—'

'Er, hi…' said the Doctor, interrupting the Mayor mid-sentence. 'Remember me? Name's the Doctor. We met in your office. What's happening?'

'The colony…' said Mayor Sedgefield, his eyes red with the promise of tears. 'We're off course… The Great White Spot… There's not enough room on the ships and we don't have enough life rafts…'

'Not enough rafts?' asked the Doctor. It was a pointless question, he knew that much; but even so it took a second or two for the enormity of what the Mayor had said to hit him.

'Not enough rafts…' he said again, only this time it wasn't a question. It was a cold, hard fact.

Breaking away from the Mayor and Captain Thomas, the Doctor began pacing in what little space he could find among the masses of people swarming towards the exit gates.

Jake and Vienna ran to his side.

'What is it?' asked Jake. 'What's happening?'

'I need to think!' said the Doctor, hitting himself on the head with both hands. 'Think! Thousands of people, not enough ships… Not enough *room* on the ships. Not enough *time* to get everyone on the TARDIS. Wait… The TARDIS… I could use the TARDIS to… No… That's no use…'

'Use the TARDIS to what?' asked Vienna.

'Well,' said the Doctor, and then in one breathless sentence: 'I can't use the TARDIS to tow the colony away from the storm it's anchored to Saturn if I tried pulling it away it would break up – oh COME ON!' He struck his head once more. 'Great big colony… Not enough ships… There's got to be something…'

'Er, Doctor.' It was Jake, standing at his side and tugging at his sleeve.

'Not now, Jake, I'm thinking…'

'But I think I've got an idea.'

The Doctor looked down at him.

'What's that?' he asked.

'I said I think I've got an idea.'

'Really? What?'

'The ships,' said Jake. 'There aren't any rockets on the colony. We move about using the flotation panels and the fusion candle, but the ships have got rockets.'

'Wait a minute,' said the Doctor. 'Are you thinking…?'

'Yeah,' said Jake, hesitantly. 'We could use the ships as our rockets. The ones facing north could fire their rockets to steer right, and then the ones facing south could fire *their* rockets to steer left.'

The Doctor thought about this for a second and then laughed.

'Yes! Jake… you're a genius!'

He grabbed Jake by the head and shook him vigorously, dazing the young boy, before running across the loading bay to where Captain Thomas was now guiding passengers onto his ship.

'Captain!' he shouted, over the din of the crowds and the sirens. 'Wait! I've got an idea. No… hang on… I *don't* have an idea, but that boy over there… That *genius* over there *does* have an idea.'

The Captain turned to the Doctor.

'What's that?'

'I SAID THAT GENIUS OVER THERE HAS AN IDEA.

We need you and the Captains of the other ships to use your rockets to steer the colony.'

'I'm sorry… What did you say?'

'I SAID WE NEED YOU AND THE CAPTAINS OF THE OTHER SHIPS TO USE YOUR ROCKETS TO STEER THE COLONY.'

'Steer the colony? Are you insane?'

'The colony doesn't have rockets,' said the Doctor, squeezing through the thronging crowd until he was within earshot of Captain Thomas. 'But you do. If you keep your ships moored but fire your rockets, we can steer the colony back onto its course, and away from the storm.'

The Captain frowned and bit his knuckle in concentration.

'Come on, Captain,' said the Doctor, impatiently. 'Can you cogitate a little quicker? Clock ticking and all the rest of it.'

'Yes,' said the Captain, at last. 'You know that might just work. A little like they do with the mining platforms on Neptune. Yes… That's a damned fine idea, Doctor.'

'Like I said,' said the Doctor, beaming, 'not my idea. His…'

He pointed at Jake.

'Now come on, Captain, we've got, ooh, about twenty minutes to save a few thousand people. Chop, chop!'

The Captain nodded and ran to his ship, barking orders at the crew, much to their confusion.

The Doctor turned to Mayor Sedgefield.

'Mr Mayor... Did you catch any of that?'

'I... er... Yes. I think so. Spaceships as rockets?'

'Then tell the other captains.'

'Of course...'

'*Now.*'

As the Mayor left them and called out to the captains of the other ships, the Doctor turned to Jake and Vienna.

'Right!' he said, 'We need to get to the control tower!'

Jake nodded.

'I think it's this way,' he said, pointing to an enormous and impossible-to-miss sign at the other end of the loading bay that read 'CONTROL TOWER'.

'Oh yeah,' said the Doctor. 'Brilliant!'

As the Doctor ran, the children joined him with their parents, still dazed and confused, following closely behind. They passed through sliding doors and climbed a narrow metal staircase that rose high above the loading bay until they came to the large, disc-shaped control room.

From its wide, semicircular windows they could look down upon the many ships that were moored at the Western Docks, including the *Pride of Deimos*, and out over the vast, pale vistas of Saturn. There, drawing ever closer, a colossal blemish on the cloudscape, was the swirling grey vortex of the Great White Spot.

'OK,' said the Doctor. 'Have you guys ever seen a boat race?'

All four members of the Carstairs family met his question with puzzled frowns.

'Right… Of course not. Never mind. OK… In a boat race there are usually four people rowing like mad and one person with a megaphone telling them to row harder. Basically, we're the person with the megaphone!'

He turned to the control desk, pressed a number of switches and buttons, and lifted up a microphone.

'Testing… testing…' he said. 'One-two. One-two. Ha! You wait your whole life to say that and then you get to do it twice on the same day. Marvellous. OK… Are you all receiving me?'

From the desk there came a number of voices, speaking in many different accents, each of them responding that they could hear him loud and clear.

'OK,' said the Doctor. '*Pride of Deimos*… You're furthest south and pointing north. We need you to fire on the count of three, but take it easy. Got that?'

'Aye aye, Doctor,' said the Captain of the *Pride of Deimos*.

'One… two… three!'

At its tail end, the rockets of the *Pride of Deimos* flared into life, jets of blue and white gas erupting out into the ether. The whole colony shuddered; the abandoned plastic cups left behind by the control tower's operators bouncing on their desks. The Doctor, Jake, Vienna and their parents all braced themselves.

'Ooh,' said the Doctor. 'Bit bumpy, but it's a start. OK, Captain… Power down, or whatever it is you space captains say. Reduce thrust. Whatever.'

'Reducing thrust, Doctor.'

Looking out over the horizon, the Doctor saw the storm drawing closer still. Even with the rockets of the *Pride of Deimos* no longer firing, the colony was still shaking.

The Doctor lifted the microphone once more, but then turned to Jake. While the rest of his family were frozen in place, their expressions ones of absolute terror, Jake was smiling. The Doctor held out the microphone.

'You do it,' he said, beaming. 'Tell him to give it some welly.'

'Welly?' said Jake, taking the microphone.

'Tell him to fire on full power. Or whatever the proper term is.'

Jake frowned. 'No,' he said. 'If they fire on full power they might break free. They need to go up to about twenty per cent power, and then the *Herald of Nanking* has to give it fifteen, maybe sixteen per cent.'

The Doctor looked from Jake to the ships down on the Docks and then back to Jake again.

'What?' he said. 'Which one's the *Herald of Nanking*?'

'That one down there,' said Jake, pointing.

'How do you know that?'

Mr Carstairs laughed.

'The ships,' he said, smiling proudly. 'He's always watching the ships.'

'Brilliant!' said the Doctor. 'Well, you seem to know what you're doing. I'll… er… just, you know… moral support and all the rest of it.'

Jake laughed and, lifting the microphone to his mouth, said, 'OK, *Pride of Deimos*, if you could go up to twenty per cent power.'

'I'm sorry,' said the Captain, 'but who *is* this?'

The Doctor leaned in to the microphone.

'I wouldn't argue,' he said. 'He knows more about all this than I do, and that's saying something.'

'Fair enough,' said the Captain. 'Rockets firing on twenty per cent.'

The rockets fired up once again and the colony shook even more violently than before.

'OK,' said Jake. '*Herald of Nanking*, if you could go up to fifteen per cent.'

Below the *Pride of Deimos*, the rockets of a smaller ship let out a fiery jet, and the whole colony began to tilt north.

'Ooh,' said the Doctor. 'Easy…'

Beyond the windows of the control tower, the storm was almost upon them. As much as the *Pride of Deimos* and *Herald of Nanking* were pushing them away, the Great White Spot was pulling them in.

'It's not enough,' said the Doctor anxiously. 'It's not *enough*. OK, Jake… I think we need to try all of them.'

'All of them?'

'All of them.'

'OK…' said Jake, nervously. 'Um… Can all of the Captains whose ships are facing north… Can you all fire your rockets? *Pride of Deimos*… go up to twenty-five per cent. *Herald of Nanking*… Go up to twenty…'

One by one Jake named the ships that lined the Western Docks and gave each captain the order to fire their rockets, telling each one in turn the exact amount of power to apply.

With a colossal roar and a blinding flash of light, the rockets of a dozen ships erupted. The colony shuddered and shook; anything that wasn't fixed into place tumbling and crashing to the floor.

Through the windows, beyond the edges of the colony, the Doctor watched as the storm came closer and closer.

Jake's plan was working. A colony the size of a small city was drifting north, the storm now veering sharply to the southernmost edges of Chelsea 426.

The flotation panel on the southwest corner began to dip violently as it drew nearer to the storm itself and they could hear a metallic groan as its fixtures were strained by the sheer force of the storm's tremendous pull.

'Come on…' said the Doctor. 'Come on!'

Bolts and rivets the size of tree trunks were wrenched free from the flotation panel's moorings and sent spinning into the storm in a glittering metallic cloud of shrapnel. The colony shook again and, with a monstrous crash, the panel was torn away and flung out into the storm, where it buckled and folded, its membrane torn to shreds and its frame smashed into tiny pieces.

'Whoops,' said the Doctor. 'That's not good.'

Still, the rockets of the ships on the Western Dock fired full blast into the face of the storm, and still the colony drifted north. The Doctor watched as they passed around the northern edges of the vortex, missing it by only a few short miles. The colony continued to shudder and shake until finally, the storm now behind them, it came to rest. The rockets of the ships below had died down.

The Doctor took the microphone from Jake.

'Er, Captains…' he said. 'What's happened?'

It was Captain Thomas who answered.

'Run out of fuel, Doctor,' he replied. 'That's the trouble, firing in the upper atmosphere. The old fuel cells aren't designed to do it. Any news yet on whether we've averted disaster?'

The Doctor grimaced.

'Not sure,' he said. 'We lost one of the flotation panels.'

There was a long pause.

The Doctor turned to Jake, Vienna and Mr and Mrs Carstairs, anxiously biting his lower lip, but noticed that none of them seemed as concerned as he was.

'Is that all?' said Captain Thomas, after an age. 'Good thing these things remain stable with just the three, then, isn't it?'

The Doctor laughed, more out of relief than anything else.

'Stable on three?' he said, still laughing.

'Oh yes. That's the thing with flotation panels. Damned things break all the time.'

'Stable on three!' said the Doctor. 'We're stable on three!'

He turned to Jake and Vienna.

'D'you hear that? We're stable on three!'

'Yeah,' said Vienna, sarcastically. 'You didn't know that?'

The Doctor's smile changed instantly into a disgruntled scowl.

'Oh, all right, Miss I-Know-Everything!' He turned to Jake. 'How do you put up with her?'

Jake smiled, and the Doctor laughed, grinning at the twins, and then at their parents.

'Your children,' he said. 'They're brilliant. Just brilliant. Did you know that? Well, of course you knew that. They're your kids. And they're brilliant!'

TWENTY

They had never, in their two years living on Chelsea 426, seen the hotel this busy. The lobby was filled with people, the passengers from those ships that had steered the colony away from the storm. Among the many new faces, Mr Carstairs made a beeline for two in particular.

'Jenny!' he called. 'Zack!'

'Oh, hello,' said Jenny. 'Apparently it's going to be three or four days before they can refuel. We were wondering if—'

'Of course!' said Mr Carstairs. 'Of course!'

His wife appeared at his side.

'The usual rate is sixty credits a night,' she said.

Mr Carstairs shook his head.

HURON PUBLIC LIBRARY
521 DAKOTA AVE S
HURON, SD 57350

'No,' he said. 'Not for these two. They can stay on the house.'

'But—'

'No, Bess,' said Mr Carstairs. 'It's the least we can do. Those ships could have left us, you know.'

Mrs Carstairs smiled.

'Yes, Brian,' she said. 'Quite right.'

She turned to Zack and Jenny.

'Welcome to the Grand Hotel. Breakfast is served between six-thirty and nine-thirty. Our son will help you with your luggage.'

She looked around the lobby for Jake.

'Jake?' she called out. 'Jake? Oh, where is he now?'

From the windows of room 237, Jake Carstairs looked down at the south-west corner of the colony.

Engineers in spacesuits were already carrying out emergency repairs to the areas of broken, jagged metal where the flotation panel had been torn away, but the Great White Spot was far behind them.

A short time earlier, some people from the colony's hospital had come to take away the Major's body, but Jake had wiped away his tears and kept what his father called a 'stiff upper lip'. Only when they had gone and he was alone in the room did he allow himself to cry.

On the other side of the room, the door of the TARDIS opened, and the Doctor stepped out.

'Are you leaving us?' Jake asked, mopping up the last

tears with his fingers and wiping his nose on the back of his hand.

'Soon,' said the Doctor. 'Thought I'd go and say goodbye to your parents first.'

Jake nodded thoughtfully.

'Where will you go?'

'Oh,' said the Doctor. 'Here and there. Anywhere, really.'

'So you can go anywhere in that thing?' asked Jake, nodding toward the TARDIS.

'Oh yeah,' said the Doctor. 'More or less.'

Jake looked back to the TARDIS.

'And do you ever take people with you? When you're travelling around?'

'Sometimes,' said the Doctor.

'Oh, right,' said Jake. 'Because I was wondering—'

The Doctor shook his head.

'No,' he said, smiling gently. 'I know what you're thinking, and no.'

'But why not?'

'Because,' said the Doctor, 'for one thing I've had my fair share of angry mothers lately, and I don't think I'd survive the wrath of yours. And for another thing...'

Jake's shoulders slumped and he hung his head.

'Look,' said the Doctor, 'life here isn't all *that* bad, is it?'

'You don't live here,' replied Jake. 'With their boring *Colony Code* and their *Mr This* and *Mrs That*. It's *boring*.

And everyone's *weird*.'

'Yeah,' said the Doctor. 'But everyone's a little bit weird, aren't they? Just a little bit. I mean… Look at you. Thirteen years old, but you know a *scary* amount about rockets. I mean, seriously. And your sister… With computers? Freaks, the pair of you.'

Jake laughed, and the Doctor smiled gently.

'I've got a feeling things are going to be a little bit different from now on,' he said. 'Don't get me wrong, it's not going to turn into the Party Capital of Saturn, but things will be different. You'll see. Besides… You've got plenty of time to see the universe. I reckon you'll make a good pilot one day.'

'You reckon?'

'Oh yeah,' said the Doctor. 'Jake Carstairs… Space Captain. Sounds perfect.'

Jake smiled.

'Come on,' the Doctor continued. 'Let's get you back to your mum and dad. Looks like they've got plenty of customers to deal with.'

The woman with the pearl earrings and necklace rolled her eyes and drummed her fingers impatiently on the reception desk.

'Come along, dear,' she said. 'I would very much like to check into my room as soon as possible, thank you. And *where* is my luggage? Really… I don't know *why* we had to take our things off the ship. I've got a perfectly acceptable cabin on the *Pride of Deimos*, you know. It has a balcony. Do *your* rooms have balconies?'

'No, madam,' replied Vienna, writing down the woman's details but scarcely daring to look up at her, fearing another glowering sneer from their guest.

'No,' said the woman. 'Of course not. A week without a balcony. I shall be writing a stern letter to the travel agents about this, you mark my words. Not allowed back on the ship… It's health and safety gone *mad* if you ask me…'

'Er, Vienna?'

Vienna looked up and saw, standing beside the woman in pearls, Wallace.

'Hi, Wallace,' she said. 'I'm a bit busy at the moment.'

'Yeah,' said Wallace. 'Sorry about that. I was just wondering… if maybe you'd, er… well, like to go see a film or something.'

'What? Now?'

'No… Not *now*, obviously. But later. When you're a bit less… well… *busy*.'

Vienna stopped writing for a moment and smiled.

'Yeah,' she said. 'Yeah, I'd like that.'

'Cool!' said Wallace, his face lighting up.

Realising that he'd spoken a little louder than planned, he nodded sheepishly.

'Cool,' he said, more quietly. 'I'll call you. Later on, I mean.'

'Yeah,' said Vienna, still beaming.

Wallace waved goodbye and walked out onto Tunbridge Street with what looked very much like a skip in his step.

Behind the desk, hidden from the view of their guests and her parents, Vienna drummed her feet excitedly on the ground, and then, taking a deep breath, wrote down the last of the pearl-wearing woman's details, and gave her the key card for her room.

'And where is the bellboy?' asked the woman, flaring her nostrils.

'Oh, right…' said Vienna, looking around the lobby. She saw, beyond the sea of guests, her brother and the Doctor stepping out of the elevator.

'Jake!' she called. 'We've got guests. Lots of guests. Can you take this lady's luggage up to room one-three-five?'

Jake nodded dutifully and jogged over to the guest and her luggage.

'This way, madam!' he said, wheeling her suitcases towards the elevators.

Vienna turned to the Doctor.

'Are you going?' she asked. There was a hint of disappointment in her tone which he hadn't quite expected.

'Yeah,' said the Doctor. 'Well… Looks like you're going to need as many free rooms as you can get.'

'Yeah,' Vienna laughed. She bit her lower lip softly, and said, 'Doctor… I'm sorry if I was a bit… you know… snappy with you earlier. And I'm sorry I called you weird.'

'Snappy?' said the Doctor. 'Oh… No. You weren't snappy. It's called *cautious*. I mean… Strange bloke turns up and starts talking about aliens… I'd be exactly the same in your shoes. Besides which, I *am* weird, so you weren't wrong there.'

Vienna laughed.

'Anyway,' the Doctor continued, 'where's your mum and dad?'

Vienna pointed past the guests to where they stood, her father with his arm around her mother's shoulder.

The Doctor crossed the lobby to join them.

'Right,' he said. 'I'll be making a move now.'

'So soon?' said Mrs Carstairs. 'But we've hardly got to know you, Doctor. I'm afraid I was a little out of sorts, earlier. Can't remember a thing about it…'

'No,' said the Doctor. 'Probably for the best. Still… Nice to see the hotel so busy.'

'Yes,' said Mr Carstairs, pensively.

'Oh,' said the Doctor. 'You don't exactly seem over the moon about it. Or should that be *moons* if you're on Saturn?'

'Well,' replied Mr Carstairs, 'it's busy *now*, Doctor, but it won't always be like this. We've given it some thought. The cruise ship companies are paying for the rooms. Compensation, apparently. We'll turn a tidy profit this week. Enough to pay for tickets back to Earth.'

The Doctor nodded.

'So you're going back, then?'

'Yes,' said Mrs Carstairs. 'Perhaps we were a little hasty in dismissing it so…' She paused to find the right word.

'Hastily?' the Doctor suggested.

'Well, quite,' said Mrs Carstairs. 'I doubt there is any place that's truly a utopia. Do you agree, Doctor?'

'Oh, absolutely,' replied the Doctor. 'I know it for a fact. Well… I should be going.'

'Goodbye, Doctor,' said Mr Carstairs, shaking the Doctor's hand. 'And thank you.'

The Doctor nodded without saying another word, and made his way back to the elevators.

Closing the door of the TARDIS behind him, the Doctor crossed the console room and leaned against the central unit on both hands. Turning a number of dials, he tuned one of the screens to a local news bulletin. Amidst the stories of the colony's invasion and its near-collision with the Great White Spot, he saw a smaller headline:

WAR HERO TO BE GIVEN FULL MILITARY
FUNERAL ON EARTH

He opened up the story in full and read it. It ran:

The body of Field Marshal Sir Henry Whittington-

Smythe, who, tragically, was killed during the incident on Saturn's Chelsea 426 colony, will be returned to Earth where he will receive a full military funeral, it has been announced. Sir Henry, a veteran of the Martian Wars, the Battle of Mercutio 14, and the Siege of the Hexion Gates, is survived by his fourteen children and thirty-six grandchildren.

'Field Marshal?' said the Doctor. '*Field Marshal?* Ha! Not a Major! He wasn't a Major! I knew he was fibbing. I could just tell.'

He shook his head, still laughing, and turned off the screen. The console room was silent now and, but for the Doctor, quite empty.

He thought about what Jake had asked him, or at least very nearly asked him, and wondered whether he had made the right decision. After all, the TARDIS being the TARDIS, he could have taken him away to see another world, another *time*, and still been able to bring him back in time for dinner.

No, he decided. He *had* done the right thing. Besides, he liked his own company. There was nothing wrong with travelling alone. No one to answer to, nobody to nag him or question him. He quite liked it, in fact. Couldn't be happier.

It was just that the TARDIS could seem a very empty place sometimes. Empty and very quiet. He could talk to the TARDIS, and often did, but it never answered back, at least never with words.

He sighed and took a deep breath.

'Right!' he said aloud. 'Where were we going? Oh yeah… Paris. 1922. The Majestic Hotel. Time to apologise to Marcel, I reckon…'

He paused, his hand still gripping the lever.

'Actually,' he said, 'I think I've had enough of hotels for a little while. Maybe some other time. Let's go for pot luck, shall we?'

He pulled the lever, turned a dial and hit a button with a triumphant thump.

The glowing transparent columns in the centre of the console rose and fell, accompanied by a metallic roar, and, with that, he was gone.

TWENTY-ONE

The monstrous black ship had come to the very edges of the solar system, driving on past the spectral Oort Cloud, with its trillions of icy fragments faintly glittering in the dim light of a distant sun.

In his quarters, General Kade stood before the sample of the Rutan plant, still housed beneath its glass dome. He was pleased that he had managed to rescue it before the colony was completely destroyed. It would be heralded as a key victory by many back on Sontar, even if those in the Battle Fleet failed to appreciate its significance. The higher ranks would clamour to see it; something which satisfied him tremendously.

Leaving his rooms and making his way to the bridge, Kade passed several of his crew, all of whom stopped in their tracks and saluted him. Though Sontarans were rarely anything less than respectful of their superior officers, it seemed that they were making an extra effort in the aftermath of their experience on the human colony.

Perhaps, Kade considered, it was a respect inspired, in part, by his victory over Colonel Sarg. That too was satisfying.

On the bridge, the crew were plotting the coordinates that would take them to their home world. The mood there was almost impossible to gauge. Surely they would appreciate that the Rutan threat had passed, almost without incident. The humans and Rutans alike had, no doubt, been consigned to the destructive cyclone of Saturn's greatest storm, just as he had assured them. All the same, he could sense dissatisfaction, even if no one dared voice it. Too many of them had been defeated by the Rutans in direct combat. Theirs was, perhaps, a hollow victory.

As Kade stepped out onto the bridge the crew stood and saluted him in unison.

'At ease,' said the General, taking to his position at the head of the bridge. He turned now to his chief navigator.

'Commander Strom,' he barked, and the commander saluted him once more. 'Have we plotted our course to Sontar?'

'We have, sir.'

HURON PUBLIC LIBRARY
521 DAKOTA AVE S
HURON, SD 57350

'Excellent, then prepare to enter hyperspace immediately.'

'Yes, sir,' replied Strom, with enthusiasm. 'That would be agreeable.'

Acknowledgements

Thanks firstly to everyone at BBC Wales and BBC Books, namely Edward Russell, Gary Russell, Justin Richards and Steve Tribe, all of them indispensable fountains of knowledge and advice (not to mention suppliers of Sontaran episode DVDs. Yes, Edward – that's you). Special hugs and kisses, also, to Lee Binding for designing another great cover!

Personal thanks to Benjamin K. Flambards (aka Lord Tinlegs), my trusty sounding board and the organiser of my 'Who-Mitzvah', and to Ceri Young for his helpful tips on Latin. And lastly, thanks to Terrance Dicks and the late Robert Holmes for creating such great villains to play around with, and to Russell T Davies, David Tennant and all the writers of the show, for making the writing of this book so much fun.

Also available from BBC Books
featuring the Doctor and Rose
as played by Christopher Eccleston and Billie Piper:

DOCTOR · WHO

Also available from BBC Books
featuring the Doctor and Rose
as played by David Tennant and Billie Piper:

THE STONE ROSE
by Jacqueline Rayner

THE FEAST OF THE DROWNED
by Stephen Cole

THE RESURRECTION CASKET
by Justin Richards

THE NIGHTMARE OF BLACK ISLAND
by Mike Tucker

THE ART OF DESTRUCTION
by Stephen Cole

THE PRICE OF PARADISE
by Colin Brake

Also available from BBC Books
featuring the Doctor and Martha
as played by David Tennant and Freema Agyeman:

DOCTOR · WHO

STING OF THE ZYGONS
by Stephen Cole

THE LAST DODO
by Jacqueline Rayner

WOODEN HEART
by Martin Day

FOREVER AUTUMN
by Mark Morris

SICK BUILDING
by Paul Magrs

WETWORLD
by Mark Michalowski

WISHING WELL
by Mark Morris

THE PIRATE LOOP
by Simon Guerrier

PEACEMAKER
by James Swallow

MARTHA IN THE MIRROR
by Justin Richards

SNOWGLOBE 7
by Mike Tucker

THE MANY HANDS
by Dale Smith

THE STORY OF MARTHA
by Dan Abnett
with David Roden,
Steve Lockley & Paul Lewis,
Robert Shearman
and Simon Jowett

Also available from BBC Books
featuring the Doctor and Donna
as played by David Tennant and Catherine Tate:

DOCTOR·WHO

GHOSTS OF INDIA
by Mark Morris

THE DOCTOR TRAP
by Simon Messingham

SHINING DARKNESS
by Mark Michalowski

BEAUTIFUL CHAOS
by Gary Russell

Also available from BBC Books
featuring the Doctor
as played by David Tennant:

DOCTOR · WHO

The Eyeless

by Lance Parkin

ISBN 978 1 846 07562 9

£6.99

At the heart of the ruined city of Arcopolis is the Fortress.
It's a brutal structure placed here by one of the sides in
a devastating intergalactic war that's long ended. Fifteen
years ago, the entire population of the planet was killed in
an instant by the weapon housed deep in the heart of the
Fortress. Now only the ghosts remain.

The Doctor arrives, and determines to fight his way
past the Fortress's automatic defences and put the
weapon beyond use. But he soon discovers he's not the
only person in Arcopolis. What is the true nature of
the weapon? Is the planet really haunted? Who are the
Eyeless? And what will happen if they get to the weapon
before the Doctor?

The Doctor has a fight on his hands. And this time he's all
on his own.

Also available from BBC Books
featuring the Doctor
as played by David Tennant:

DOCTOR·WHO

Judgement of the Judoon

by Colin Brake

ISBN 978 1 846 07639 8

£6.99

Elvis the King Spaceport has grown into the sprawling
city-state of New Memphis – an urban jungle, where
organised crime is rife. But the launch of the new
Terminal 13 hasn't been as smooth as expected. And
things are about to get worse...

When the Doctor arrives, he finds the whole terminal
locked down. The notorious Invisible Assassin is at work
again, and the Judoon troopers sent to catch him will stop
at nothing to complete their mission.

With the assassin loose on the mean streets of New
Memphis, the Doctor is forced into a strange alliance.
Together with teenage private eye Nikki and a ruthless
Judoon Commander, the Doctor soon discovers that
things are even more complicated – and dangerous – than
he first thought…

Also available from BBC Books
featuring the Doctor
as played by David Tennant:

DOCTOR · WHO

The Slitheen Excursion

by Simon Guerrier

ISBN 978 1 846 07640 4

£6.99

1500BC – King Actaeus and his subjects live in mortal fear of the awesome gods who have come to visit their kingdom in ancient Greece. Except the Doctor, visiting with university student June, knows they're not gods at all. They're aliens.

For the aliens, it's the perfect holiday – they get to tour the sights of a primitive planet and even take part in local customs. Like gladiatorial games, or hunting down and killing humans who won't be missed.

With June's enthusiastic help, the Doctor soon meets the travel agents behind this deadly package holiday company – his old enemies the Slitheen. But can he bring the Slitheen excursion to an end without endangering more lives? And how are events in ancient Greece linked to a modern-day alien plot to destroy what's left of the Parthenon?

Also available from BBC Books
featuring the Doctor
as played by David Tennant:

DOCTOR·WHO

Prisoner of the Daleks
by Trevor Baxendale
ISBN 978 1 846 07641 1
£6.99

The Daleks are advancing, their empire constantly
expanding into Earth's space. The Earth forces are resisting
the Daleks in every way they can. But the battles rage on
across countless solar systems. And now the future of our
galaxy hangs in the balance…

The Doctor finds himself stranded on board a starship
near the frontline with a group of ruthless bounty hunters.
Earth Command will pay them for every Dalek they kill,
every eye stalk they bring back as proof.

With the Doctor's help, the bounty hunters achieve the
ultimate prize: a Dalek prisoner – intact, powerless, and
ready for interrogation. But where the Daleks are involved,
nothing is what it seems, and no one is safe. Before long
the tables will be turned, and how will the Doctor survive
when he becomes a prisoner of
the Daleks?

Also available from BBC Books
featuring the Doctor
as played by David Tennant:

DOCTOR·WHO

Autonomy

by Daniel Blythe

ISBN 978 1 846 07759 3

£6.99

Hyperville is 2013's top high-tech 24-hour entertainment complex – a sprawling palace of fun under one massive roof. You can go shopping, or experience the excitement of Doomcastle, WinterZone, or Wild West World. But things are about to get a lot more exciting – and dangerous…

What unspeakable horror is lurking on Level Zero of Hyperville? And what will happen when the entire complex goes over to Central Computer Control?

For years, the Nestene Consciousness has been waiting and planning, recovering from its wounds. But now it's ready, and its deadly plastic Autons are already in place around the complex. Now more than ever, visiting Hyperville will be an unforgettable experience…

Also available from BBC Books
featuring the Doctor
as played by David Tennant:

DOCTOR · WHO

The Krillitane Storm

by Christopher Cooper

ISBN 978 1 846 07761 6

£6.99

When the TARDIS materialises in medieval Worcester,
the Doctor finds the city seemingly deserted. He soon
discovers its population are living in a state of terror,
afraid to leave their homes after dark, for fear of meeting
their doom at the hands of the legendary Devil's
Huntsman.

For months, people have been disappearing, and the
Sheriff has imposed a strict curfew across the city,
his militia maintaining control over the superstitious
populace with a firm hand, closing the city to outsiders.
Is it fear of attack from beyond the city walls that drives
him or the threat closer to home? Or does the Sheriff have
something to hide?

After a terrifying encounter with a deadly Krillitane, the
Doctor realises the city has good reason to be scared.

Also available from BBC Books:

DOCTOR·WHO

MONSTERS AND VILLAINS
by Justin Richards

ALIENS AND ENEMIES
by Justin Richards

CREATURES AND DEMONS
by Justin Richards

STARSHIPS AND SPACESTATIONS
by Justin Richards

THE SHOOTING SCRIPTS
by Russell T Davies,
Mark Gatiss, Robert Shearman,
Paul Cornell and Steven Moffat

THE INSIDE STORY
by Gary Russell

THE ENCYCLOPEDIA
by Gary Russell

THE TIME TRAVELLER'S ALMANAC
by Steve Tribe

Also available from BBC Books:

DOCTOR·WHO

Companions and Allies

by Steve Tribe

ISBN 978 1 846 07749 4

£7.99

The Doctor has been travelling through space and time for centuries, showing his friends and companions the wonders of the universe. From Sarah Jane Smith and the Brigadier to Martha Jones and Donna Noble, *Companions and Allies* celebrates the friends who have been by his side and the heroes that have helped him battle his deadliest foes. Find out:

- How the First Doctor uprooted schoolteachers Ian and Barbara from their twentieth-century lives
- Why the Third Doctor worked for UNIT
- How the Fifth Doctor sacrificed his life for Peri
- Who helped the Eighth Doctor save Earth from the Master
- What became of Rose Tyler and her family

And much more. Beautifully illustrated and including – for the first time – a complete story guide to the adventures of all ten Doctors, this is the definitive guide to the Doctor's intergalactic family.

Coming soon from BBC Books:

DOCTOR·WHO

The Ultimate Monster Guide

by Justin Richards
ISBN 978 1 846 07745 6
£14.99

With *The Ultimate Monster Guide*, *Doctor Who* historian Justin Richards has created the most comprehensive guide to the Doctor's enemies ever published. With fully illustrated entries that cover everything from Adipose and Autons to Zarbi and Zygons, this guide tells you everything you need to know about the many dastardly creatures the Doctor has fought since he first appeared on television.

Featuring a wealth of material from the current and classic series, the guide also includes behind-the-scenes secrets of how the monsters were created, as well as design drawings and images. Find out how the Cybermen were redesigned over the years, and how Davros was resurrected to lead his Daleks once again. Discover the computer magic that made the Beast possible, and the make-up wizardry that created the Weeping Angels. Learn how many incarnations of the Master the Doctor has encountered, and which other misguided Time Lords he has defeated...

Lavishly designed with photos and artwork throughout, *The Ultimate Monster Guide* is essential reading for all travellers in time and space!